Doug Liberty Presents Bandit the Dancing Raccoon

<u>a novel</u>

by John L. Sheppard

Paragraph Line Books
Oakland, California

Doug Liberty Presents Bandit the Dancing Raccoon:
a novel

Copyright © 2018 by John Lawrence Sheppard

First Printing: 2018
PL 124

ISBN 978-1-942086-12-3

Paragraph Line Books
Oakland, California

www.paragraphline.com
www.johnlsheppard.com

Dang me, dang me
They oughta take a rope and hang me
High from the highest tree
Woman, would you weep for me?
—Roger Miller

We come into the world alone and we die alone. Why, in life, should we be any less alone?
—Diogenes the Cynic

Also by John L. Sheppard

After the Jump
Sometimes Fatal Events Have Occurred
Explosive Decompression
Escape from Mondo Tiki Island
White Trash Lotto

Out of print titles are available for free at
www.johnlsheppard.com

For Nancy

SEE FAILURE AS A BEGINNING, NOT AN END

It is not kind of you all to point out that I am drinking at an Alcoholics Anonymous meeting in this here get-sober hospital. I am well aware that I'm drinking. I am also well aware that I've gone over the time limit, even though there doesn't seem to be any time limit posted in this meeting room. Or a clock! Shouldn't you put one next to the sugar donuts over there?

You can keep your no-drink chip. And you're free to get up and leave if you want. I'm going to stand at this podium and bloviate until I'm finished. Go already! Why are you still here? It's probably for the same reason you all slow down and take a lingering look when there's a crash on the freeway.

Yes, I am a human crash on the freeway. That's what I am. Also, I'm a non-practicing heterosexual.

Every night, when I attempt to sleep, I hear the car crash that took my family from me, that I caused as a six-year-old boy. I hear my family screaming, and the screech of metal, and my mama screaming over the top of it, "Tris! Tris!" There's a thought in there from her, unarticulated, but articulated just the same. It's aimed at a six-year-old killer.

Shortly before the accident, I irritated my father, and when he swung around to hit me, he drove us over the median of the freeway. Nothing good can happen when you drive over the median of a freeway and I can assure you in this particular instance nothing good came of it. By the next day, my mother, my father and my two siblings had passed into the great beyond. I remained here on this earthly plane. I wasn't even hurt all that much. I have no scars from the accident. I merely have the sound of their screams on constant replay in my head forever.

When I was 13, when I had my first jolt of hormones, I stopped sleeping so much at night. I could hear them, could hear it all. It is my only real memory of my family. No visuals, just sound. And that sound lives inside my head as a keening scream. It's the last moment of their lives, trapped in gray matter. I hate it. I treasure it. The drink dulls the edges of it. Somewhat. But not all the way. Oh, no. No matter how drunk I get, it never, ever goes away.

But sober. Sober is no way to live.

I'm gonna make me a waffle blazer when I get home, if I have a home. I may not have a home. Maybe the bank or the county tax assessor's office took the house while I was stuck here in the get-sober hospital.

So... how to construct a blazer made of waffles?

For one thing, I'm not sewing together a bunch of Eggo waffles, or even the square kind. I need a big-ass waffle iron in the shape of the front panels of this waffle blazer. Back panels, too. And, of course, lapels and pockets. You need pockets in your waffle blazer. I need lots of batter.

So once I've got all the panels done, I'll glue them together with maple syrup that has been boiled down into a thick gluey paste.

It's a blazer, so it needs a patch on the front pocket. A coat of arms. I think I'll carve up a few strawberries. Maybe make a strawberry lion, extending his strawberry paws, with a little strawberry crown on his head.

I need a boutonnière. I'll carve it out of a disk of butter so it looks like a white carnation. I'll put a couple of peppermint leaves behind it.

I need a pocket square. I'll carve up and sand down a piece of pecan brittle and slide it into the waffle pocket.

I will wear my waffle blazer proudly. And when I am done wearing it, I will eat it proudly.

I am a 41 regular.

In retrospect, life is a series of ill-fitting clothes, unsatisfying meals and too-long periods of sobriety.

And adventures—good, bad and otherwise. Now, sit back you drunks. I'm going to tell a story here. Get comfortable. This is about an adventure, and, like most of my adventures, this one was not planned.

My plan that evening was to drink myself to sleep. I'm at my best when asleep. One of my two ex-wives told me that. Can't remember which one.

It was the dry season in Florida, so I could open the windows and allow the wall of noise—mostly insects, and creatures that eat them, buzzing and croaking their lungs out—to settle into my room, an accompaniment to the interior death scream tinnitus and to the heavy buzz of alcohol in my system. As I drifted off, I heard the dull thump of an animal flinging open my trash can. The can was one of those garbage company-issued dealies, tall and green plastic with black wheels attached at the bottom, a flip-open lid on top.

I was grieving two deaths, my maternal grandparents, the ones who raised me, who had brought me up in the house I was occupying. They weren't long gone at this point. One died of cancer, the other died in an accident.

They were my last attachments to this world. Not that I was all that attached to begin with.

My grandfather built the house himself back in the 1970's, before all the hurricane codes were written. It was a rickety place made of bowing pine planks, crumbling particle board, bendy nails, frayed shoelaces and used chewing gum.

Thump, thump, went the trash can. I reached under my sagging twin bed and found my grandfather's double-barreled shotgun.

The insects, birds and reptiles all stopped humming for a moment, and then started up again. My heart leapt in my chest, it was all I could hear in that moment. That, and, let's face it, that keening noise emanating from the middle of my brain. But, hey... maybe it was Bigfoot! Or what do we call him down here? The Florida Swamp Ape! It felt like my thrumming heart was pierced through with needles. Maybe I shouldn't go out there, I thought. Maybe whatever it is should be left alone. My instincts told me to go outside and confront it, to be a man for once in my life, to face whatever creature this was head-on.

My instincts have never served me particularly well.

I headed outside. I walked out of my room into the hallway, then into the living room, then into the laundry room, and then into the garage, barefoot. I stepped on a pricker from a pricker bush, hopped up and down on one foot, leaned the shotgun against the wall and pulled the pricker out. "C'mon," I said to myself. "Let's do this. Let's do this right. Let's defend the ol' property. Be a manly man." I picked up the shotgun and quietly walked to the door separating the garage from the concrete pad containing the undersized air conditioner unit and the trash can filled with garbage I meant to defend. I pulled the door open quickly, and a rush of moist air washed over me, along with the stench from the open trash can. I lifted the gun and leveled it at a raccoon with a burnt potato wedge in his mouth. He stopped masticating. He let the potato wedge drop.

I was about to shoot the raccoon when I noticed two things: One, he was wearing a collar with a shiny metal tag attached. Two, he had his hands raised.

Fine. I lowered the shotgun, he lowered his hands. My heart stopped racing. I felt a cool drip of relief spreading through my chest instead.

Now he was using sign language. What the ever-lovin' hell was going on? Was I trapped in a dream of some sort?

"I don't understand sign language," I told him.

So he warbled out two words, "Playyyy 'Freee-birrrrd.'"

"Follow me," I said.

This was clearly a mistake. I had yet to discover that you shouldn't invite a raccoon into your house, even if he did have a taste for southern rock and french fries.

He free-climbed down off the trash can and followed me through the garage and into the laundry room. He peered around, snorted contemptuously, and then spied the kitchen. He climbed up on a barstool next to the kitchen counter. I'd been eating my dinner every night over the sink and decided that I'd like to sit down while doing that, so I'd bought a single barstool at K-mart.

I made him a peanut butter sandwich. That's what I'd been eating for dinner ever since I'd run out of cash. I was trying to sell my grandparents' home. I'd had a couple of offers, but the dump couldn't seem to make it past a simple home inspection. I had no money to improve the place. At some point, property taxes would come due and then I'd be out on my ass.

The raccoon held the sandwich with both of his little hands and quickly gobbled his way through it. I turned the spigot on and he drank from it. He wiped his little hands off on his pelt. I cracked open my last beer, a Natty Ice, and we each took a swig.

I went to my bedroom and brought out my iPad. I'd been stealing my neighbor's WiFi, and he still hadn't changed his password from his last name. I poked around on YouTube, and played the raccoon some Lynyrd Skynyrd.

He danced on the kitchen counter, and even did a little bit of air guitar. I pulled out my iPhone and filmed him for a few minutes, and posted it to YouTube. I had an account there from a Talking Heads cover band I'd been the lead singer for—Stop Making Cents. All of us in the band had been employees of Buy and Bye, and we all wore our green work polo shirts and khakis as part of the act until we were served a restraining order.

After a half hour of aerobics, the raccoon tired, stopped, slumped to the counter and closed his eyes.

I poked him in the side with my index finger. He was skin and bones under all that fur. "You okay?"

He waved his little hand at me dismissively. I picked him up gingerly and carried him to the old master bedroom where I put him up for the night, his raccoon head where my grandmother's head had once rested on the pillow. The double bed where he slept had been, up until a few days before that night, where my grandparents had slept. I crept out of the room and quietly closed the door.

I neglected to read the tag on his collar. I should have. Maybe it would have solved the problem right away, before he became a problem. A multitude of problems.

I went to bed and slept for the first time in weeks. There was something about taking care of that raccoon that had unlocked sleep for me.

I blinked awake in the morning, sat up, and realized that I'd allowed a wild animal to stay in the house, under the same roof as me. I sat up quickly and raced to the bedroom, threw open the door.

He'd torn the bedroom to shreds. The wall-to-wall carpet was ripped into strips. The double bed had a hole in the center of it the size of a football, with mattress foam flung in all directions. The walls were scratched knee-high down to the gypsum in the drywall.

In the master bath, I found him on the counter next to the sink staring into the mirror at himself, his little hands caressing his face.

LOVE WHAT YOU DO, OR LEAVE

I should tell you about my first wife. That might help explain why I let a raccoon in the house.

Delores had 20 years on me. Maybe more. I can't remember now. She'd been blonde once in her life, she'd told me. Then brunette. When I met her, her hair color was whatever they had on sale at the Eckerd drugstore. Something to color it and give it bounce. She was from Ohio. She didn't specify north or south. Cleveland or Cincinnati. Or maybe somewhere in between. Turned out to be Zanesville. She was pale, like me. Neither of us spent much time in the sun, despite our immersion in the subtropics. She had a mole on her cheek that looked like a chocolate chip floating in a bowl of cream of wheat.

My teeth hurt, like a young Nick Cage. My bones hurt. I was chronic. I was a complainer. She liked that about me.

I lived at home, but my parents were long dead.

Who was President? Was it Bush yet? Or was it still Clinton? There were hostages somewhere on the other side of the globe, maybe. There was a civil war in eastern Europe that we'd involved ourselves in. But 9-11 hadn't happened. Does that even sound right? Terror. Somewhere.

My fingernails were dirty. I worked grill at an 1890's-themed restaurant. Here a burn, there a burn. Everywhere a burn-burn. We featured a special sauce on our burgers, and our hot dogs were soaked in beer.

Outside it was the middle of the night, but it was still 95. Boiling. I took off my bowtie, my red-and-white-striped shirt, the straw boater. I was down to my sweat-soaked undershirt with yellow stains on the underarms, black trousers dotted with grease and white bleach stains, black oxfords that were cracked across the top and splitting across the soles, and sagging sweat socks. Something essential was oozing out of my pores, never to be recovered. The a/c on the roof sprinkled cool air through the vents above us. It sunk past our skinny bodies quickly, pooling on the white tile floor.

I watched a burger sizzle on the grill. I think it was for her. Or me.

"You look like shit," she said.

"Thanks."

"It's going to burn."

"What's your name again?"

"You exhaust me."

I flipped the burger. I reached into a drawer and found a bun. Before the other side burned, I scraped the burger up and slipped it on the bun. I handed it to her.

"Nothing on it?" She bit into it. I could sense her teeth ripping through the dry bun and the scorched burger. Fingernails on chalkboard shivers and twitches. "God." Her voice muffled by stale bun. "I'm dying."

"Nowhere to go but up."

Her waitress's uniform left much to the imagination. Shoulders to ankles frilly dress, corset in the middle, her currently auburn hair tied into a tight bun in the back, like a post-Civil War prairie schoolmarm. She finished the burger, wiped her hands on her dress, and ran her mouth against her sleeve. "You're a peach."

"Yeah." I saw myself reflected in the glass that surrounded us. Gaunt. Nothing to see here. Move along.

She pulled herself a beer out of the only tap in the joint, swirled it around in a spotty glass as if inspecting it for impurities, and daintily swigged it down with one pinkie extended on her drinking hand. She sleeved her mouth clean again and then disappeared into the back of the restaurant. I heard clinking. I heard a belch.

I wasn't a drinker yet. I hadn't had my first drink. I remember this moment and wonder, "When was it that I discovered drinking?"

Did I mention she wrote poetry? It was crap poetry. But, hey: Poetry.

Two more hours and we could leave the place to the breakfast shift.

"You're still here, huh?" Who was this? When did this conversation begin? He smiled expectantly at me, sitting at one of the four chrome stools at the counter.

"Where was I supposed to go?"

"Away."

I squinted at him. "Who are you?"

He smiled at me, this character. "We went to school together. Don't you remember?"

"College or high school?"

"You went to college? You?"

"So high school then."

"I was in the kiltie band with you. Remember? You played clarinet. I played saxophone. I sat behind you in nearly every class. Alphabetical order. English, biology. Mister Dombrowski. Remember him?" He told me his name, which I immediately forgot.

But I remembered something about him. There was a girl I tutored in high school who had a reputation for being loose. She was on the cheer squad. She was cute enough, but my taste then, as now, ran toward smart women, not girls barely passing English. She and I had a mutual disinterest in each other sexually, which was clear to both of us from the get-go. It was a relief to her to be around a boy who wasn't asking her for sex. I worked with her for a month on a couple of papers for her English class and her father paid me about $100. We'd sit at her kitchen table while her mother sat in the living room, drinking gin and 7Up out of a plastic tumbler. After a month, I gave up the whole enterprise as hopeless and got the job at the restaurant, which I held onto through the rest of high school and all the way through college. But I remembered the cop now. At a pep rally, he was seated behind me in the gym bleachers. I was bored, staring off into space, when I heard a voice behind my ear say, "You nail that?" I ignored the voice, as students in my high school rarely spoke to me. I was mostly invisible, save for the members of the kiltie band.

To be clear, I was never in the band in high school. There was a guy who looked like me who was in the band and played the clarinet. I can't remember his name either, but I was always being mistaken for my clarinet-playing doppelgänger in high school, to the point where band members would walk by me in the halls and say, "See you at band practice."

The only people who noticed me in high school, besides all the goofs who'd mistaken me for my clarinet-playing double, were teachers, who insisted on hanging a horrifying judgment on me. I had, in their estimation, potential. There is nothing worse than having potential. I would have preferred being labeled an incompetent, or a drooling idiot. But I was stuck with my potential, wore it like the carcass of a dead skunk around my neck. I would eventually rebel against it for my adult lifetime. But first came college.

Anyway, that was the future cop asking me that question. He poked my shoulder. "Hey! I said, 'Did you nail that?'" I think the implication would have been that if she'd had sex with me, she'd have sex with anyone. Which would make her a slut. Which would mean an invite to his next kegger with all his date-rape buddies.

I turned my head and looked at him. He was mustache-free at the time, but he was the same piece of work. "No," I said. "She's kind of an idiot."

"Well," he reasoned, "you wouldn't be fucking her *brain*."

So that was the guy sitting at the counter, asking me why I hadn't left Sarasota. I tried to turn the tables. "Why are *you* still here?"

He turned his head to the side, like a confused dog. He flicked the badge on his shirt. Sarasota Police Department. He had a mustache. Mustache guy, cop, Johnny Law. He was classified in my memory. I was done remembering anything else about him.

"You could have been a cop somewhere else."

"Sure." He tapped his coffee cup and I refilled it. "How old is that coffee?"

"I made it at midnight. I'll have a cup and finish it off. Then I'll make a new pot."

The countertop was black. Obsidian. It seemed mystical, like that monolith in *2001*. I looked into it for a moment and saw my face reflected up, but in black. Then I looked up at the florescent light boxes above surrounded by acoustic tile. The tile had semi-mysterious yellow stains, like there was a hobo living in the attic urinating on them.

"You were going to make new coffee."

"Right." The stainless steel machine beckoned. Next to it sat a fake potted plant. I had failed to dust the plant for the 30th day in a row. I poured myself a cup, then poured the muddy remains at the bottom of the pyrex pot into the little water sink near the counter. I dumped the old grounds in the trash and opened a little drawer where there were metallic bags in either brown or orange (decaf). I tore open a brown metallic bag with my teeth, kicking the drawer shut. Inside was a white bag, like a giant tea bag, filled with coffee. It was aromatic. I wanted to hug it to my chest. How long had it been since I'd slept at night? I tossed it into the slot on the machine and pushed a red button. I listened as new water was automagically spigotted in, and then it boiled. Brown liquid dripped down. Drip, drop. Like those old commercials. How did they go?

"Can I get that to-go?" the cop asked, standing up. He put on a service cap that also had a badge on it. He slipped a nightstick into his belt. Where had the nightstick been?

"Sure." I found a styrofoam cup and slipped the pot out from under the little brown stream and the styrofoam cup under. A little sizzle of coffee managed to splash on the hot plate and dance there for a moment before disappearing. The cup filled up and then I slipped the pot back while pulling the cup away. Neat trick—like magic, but not magic. Prestidigitation. I found a plastic lid and fit it on top of the styrofoam cup, perhaps poorly.

"Been nice catching up," the cop said with a wink and a bit of a sneer. "Be seeing you."

"Yes. Catching up."

The cop jingled out the glass door and off to his police cruiser.

Lemon-scented bug spray misted out from a box near the door. I breathed it in, deeply. I imagined tiny bugs inside my lungs, my bloodstream, dying. Pop, pop, pop. Like tiny balloons.

She slipped out of the back as the lights from the cruiser swept through the diner. "You know that cop?"

"That's his story anyway."

"When I first came here, he wanted to lock me up. Prostitution."

"Prostitution."

"It was a misunderstanding."

"Oh?"

"I offered to blow him for ten bucks. I was desperate. Living in my car with my boyfriend."

"I see."

"You don't, but it's cute that you think you do. How old are you again?"

I had to think about it for a moment. Do some math. "Twenty-two," I concluded.

"A little young to forget how old you are."

I shrugged. "I guess." I drank the old-ass coffee that I'd poured, about half the cup. Bitterness. Like death. The rest I poured down the sink. I bused away the cop's coffee cup. "Have I ever told you about the time my cousin Carwyn locked me in a porta-potty and turned it over? This was at the family reunion in Pennsylvania. I was tinted blue and smelled like shit for a month."

"Boy, he must have hated you. What did you do to him?"

"Nothing! I did nothing to him!"

"You must have done something."

"I am innocent."

She went out into the empty restaurant and sat in one of the chairs out there, staring out through the streaked windows at the night. Dust. Cobwebs. Hurricane lanterns on each table. Beige vinyl tablecloths with black cigarette burns. It was like a John Singer Sargent painting rendered by Edward Hopper.

She lit a cigarette and blew delicate rings. She was staring at her own reflection in the windows. You could see both, along with the ever-present condensation drip-dropping. And the streetlights with the bugs circling them. A car drove past on the Tamiami Trail—a Buick Century. Was it gold? Who could tell? Then it was gone.

I stood near the grill, staring at my hands. I'd been fighting the conviction that I had the ability to make my hands go through solid objects. I don't know why I was fighting my incipient insanity. Hardly seemed worth the effort.

The sun came up, our relief arrived, and it was time to leave. We slumped out the door into the moist air.

Now I remember: Clinton was still president at the time. Good to know.

I lived with my grandparents, and had since I was seven. Or six. I was young when I moved in with them, but at 22 I was, perhaps, a bit old to be living with them.

My grandfather, who I'll call "Pop," had been involved in some way in Korea, or Vietnam. Maybe the Army. I'm not sure. He hadn't really said much about it, but there was a photo on the wall above the roll top desk where he kept his checkbook. One of the helmeted boys in the photo looked like me in my twenties, except he had that hard look of someone who'd missed meals in his youth, and maybe missed out on other things.

Pop worked until he was 62 and retired with a civil service pension and a union pension. He worked for the National Council on Weights and Measures in Sarasota, but wasn't originally from Sarasota. He had contempt for Sarasotans, and for southerners in general. "The heat," he said on more than one occasion, a Hav-A-Tampa cigar clutched in his teeth, smoldering, "the heat melts their brains down here." He wouldn't shop at Publix because it was a scab joint. He was a dedicated socialist. I felt small around him, but not because he was physically enormous. We were, by the time I graduated from New College of Florida, the same size. Both our chests were sunken, concave almost, but his seemed larger. More thrust out, let's say.

Pop didn't care that I was living there with them. "In the Soviet Union, three generations of a family lived in the same small apartment. That's how they did it in civilized societies." He'd decided some time in the 1950's that the United States wasn't civilized, but the real hammer to the chest was, for him, when Ronald Reagan was reelected in 1984. "Anyone, any country, can make a mistake that big. Once. But repeating it? Well."

He was balding. I am now balding, in the future, in the same house that I shared with a raccoon, and now in this wonderful get-sober hospital, I look like Pop more than ever. He kept a trimmed beard, a Van Dyke. I think he wanted to look like Lenin. I am clean-shaven now, otherwise I'd be his spitting image.

I see him when I'm shaving. He's been dead... shit, how long has it been? A month? I'd have to check. I'll check later.

Pop was happy when I chose New College instead of going to a big university. I had offers of free tuition elsewhere, but he was insistent about dipping into his savings to send me to the little college that had been cobbled together on the former John Ringling estate. From the library—which used to be someone's house, maybe a minor Ringling, not John—I could look out on Sarasota Bay, on an orange and purple sunset, on seagulls swooping and snapping at invisible creatures bubbling to the surface of sun-dappled saltwater. New College gave out no grades, only critiques by our professors. I took an impractical major, philosophy, which Pop also applauded. I was veering away from being part of the capitalist machine, which has a habit of grinding workers' bones into dust.

Anyway, at some point, I graduated and kept the same job in the themed greasy spoon near the college, on the Tamiami Trail. Pop was thrilled about that, too. In the late 1990's, I could have wandered off to New York to become a bond trader, I suppose, even with a degree in philosophy.

I specialized in Kant (wrestled with Kant), but took an interest in the Greeks, too. My thesis (titled: *Ego A-Go-Go: An Analysis of the Bubblegum Pop of the 1960's*) was a mess, but my committee gave me a pass. They all liked me, I think. Or maybe they tolerated me. I didn't make a lot of fuss in class. I rarely got into arguments, which was unusual for a philosophy major. All we do is argue, even when we're in a room by ourselves. That's the essence of philosophy. I finished a semester early. My thesis advisor took me aside and gave me advice on how to get into Princeton. He'd gone to Princeton. I never did go to college again.

Years later, I saw my thesis advisor from New College on TV. This was after 9-11. Fox News? Or maybe it was CNN. He was one of a trio of talking heads floating in boxes around an angry host with crossed arms. I was in a hospital waiting room in Chicago. My second wife was in surgery. At the time, I wrote newsletters for a company near Chicago, and had the kind of insurance that made unethical doctors drool. "Turn it up," I said to a clerk hiding behind a sliding glass divider.

She reached over and slid the divider open. "Your wife isn't out of surgery. You mustn't be nervous." She slid it shut.

I walked over and knocked on the glass.

"Sir?" She was exasperated, but not only with me. With life. She was one of those women who should have been attractive. She had all the hallmarks of being attractive. She had a cute button nose and rosy cheeks and wavy hair that cascaded down to delicate shoulders. But she wasn't attractive. It was like someone had attached a hose to her and sucked every bit of charisma out of her body, leaving behind an ornamental husk.

"Please turn up the TV." I gestured toward the blob of squawking plastic and glass.

"Oh," she said. "Oh. Oh." She fumbled around the little desk-like area that surrounded her, there was nothing there to personalize it, and eventually she found the remote underneath a copy of *OK!* magazine. A female celebrity was on the cover. The cover said that she was living a new life. A better life. No more alcohol or drugs. The nurse aimed the remote at the TV, which was bolted to an arm that descended from a drop ceiling composed of acoustic tiles, many of them puddle-stained piss yellow, and turned up the TV. A segmented green bar at the bottom of the screen crept from one end to the other and I could hear my former thesis advisor, now a full professor at the University of Eastern Minnesota, claiming that 9-11 was an inside job.

The TV was a Westinghouse.

"Well." I looked over at the nurse with a dismissive glance.

She slid shut the sliding door, set down the remote, and began leafing through the magazine so she would not have to endure my presence any longer.

I walked back over to my chair and slumped in it.

"We have become makers of our fate when we have ceased to pose as its prophets," my former professor said, "Our knowledge can only be finite, while our ignorance must necessarily be infinite."

"It is impossible for a man to learn what he thinks he already knows," I said aloud.

I was the only one sitting in the room. I laughed. I was enjoying the reaction of the host and the other guests, who all had the expressions of people who were in a compact room when someone else farted, loudly and fragrantly, and they were not supposed to mention the smell or sound.

My grandmother. I called her "Matka." I called her that for the same reason I called Pop "Pop." I fell into it. Or she told me to call her that. Probably the latter.

After the car crash, I came to live with my mother's parents. My father's parents weren't around anymore. I think they were in California. Or maybe Colorado. They were in a "C" state out west. They were flimflam artists, just like the rest of his family. They were originally, all of my father's family, from Benzine Township, Pennsylvania, a place I loathe with intense passion. We didn't keep in touch. My father's sister had kids and they were more attached to them. There was a reason for that.

The thing is: I kind-of, sort-of caused the car crash. My mother lived long enough to blame me, and then she died. Everyone else—my sister, my brother, my father—died on site. They were dead before the emergency vehicles could arrive.

I don't want to leave any mystery here. *What isn't this guy telling me?* you're asking yourself. I don't remember much of it.

I remember Tampa General Hospital. I remember intense pain. I broke several ribs in the crash. As part of my rehabilitation, I blew into a clear plastic device and made a tiny ball levitate. There were crush injuries. Doctors don't give children pain medication that could possibly addict them. That's what a nurse told me as I sobbed. Or maybe they all heard what I'd done, how I'd killed my nuclear family, and decided to punish me for it. I was six. Did I mention that? Six!

I had a habit of reading road signs, so I always sat behind my father, who always drove. We were in a Ford Fairlane sedan. You could fit two modern sedans inside a Ford Fairlane. My father was a traveling salesman. A swindler. That was the family business: Swindling. The Ford was an immense car. This one had been painted robin's egg blue. The two front seats were bucket seats. The back seat was a bench seat and none of us were strapped in. This was in the days when people would say, "I prefer to be thrown clear," in case of an auto accident. As my mother told it, I continued to read road signs even after my father, who had a headache, shouted at me to stop. As I continued to read road signs, he turned in his seat while driving and attempted to take a swing at me. I ducked close to the door, and he drove the car over the median on the Tamiami Trail and directly into a semi carrying jelly beans. No, wait. It was a tanker transporting corn syrup to a jelly bean factory, where they made orange- and grapefruit-flavored jelly beans that were sold to tourists. My mother, before dying, said that she'd shrieked at me to shut up, that I never shut up, that I was recklessly verbose, especially around my father. I cannot picture either my mother or father. They are blanks to me now. I cannot picture my brother or sister. They are similarly blanks. I try to conjure them up on occasion. I cannot.

I can hear them screaming though. I can hear them right now. Mix that with the sound of metal scraping metal. Metal ripping. Yes, that's the sound—screaming, metal. That sound never goes away.

The thing was, we were on our way to Benzine Township, Pennsylvania, to an annual family reunion that lasted, bizarrely, throughout the month of August. There was a family compound up there and everything. There was a cousin who'd spent the previous August tormenting me because I'd seen him in a compromising position that wasn't his fault. But he didn't see it that way. I wanted to cause the crash to avoid seeing that cousin. His name was

Carwyn. That particular year, it was mission accomplished.

If you're a fan of irony, then enjoy this: Pop drove me to Pennsylvania every year after that year so I could be with my family. And every year, that cousin I was trying to avoid would find me and do unspeakable things to me. I will speak about the unspeakable things at length if someone makes a liquor run for me. I do not see a show of hands. You all must not be as thirsty as I am.

Matka took all the family albums from when I was a child and hid them thinking that the memories would be too painful for me. Or maybe seeing her dead grandchildren and dead daughter would be too painful for her.

I asked her, when I was a teenager, "Did my mother look like you? Did she look like me?"

Matka glowered at me. "This isn't an appropriate conversation." Then she got a strange look on her face. "'My mother'? Is that the way you think of her? You called her 'mama.'"

"Oh," I went. "Mama." I was trying it out. Seeing if something rose to the surface. There was nothing there. "What about my father? What did I call him?"

"Your mama accused you of being a murderer. So let's not discuss her anymore. Or your father."

"I'm curious, that's all."

"'Curious,' he says." She snorted. She was a slight woman with an athletic build. She'd been in one of the minor circuses for many years before meeting Pop. One of the Gibsonton-based ones. She roller-skated and did tricks. A capuchin monkey was involved. He wasn't the best monkey, Matka told me, but he had an expressive face, which made him a good enough monkey. His name was Chester. Her family was from overseas. Somewhere. We didn't talk about it. I assumed she was Cuban, like a lot of Floridians. There were many things that Matka didn't think were worth discussion. "Your daddy was a awful man. He beat you. Let's have no more conversation about it."

There wasn't a single photo of my father, mother, sister or brother in the house. Not one. There were many photos of me. On a wall in the Florida room, a progression of school photos tracked my progress from an unsmiling preteen to an unsmiling teen. I went from chubby to gawky. I wore identical, oversized blue-collared shirts in each photo. There was a semblance of sky in the background of each. In the junior high school photo—eighth grade, I think—I appeared to be mildly quizzical. Otherwise, the expression rarely changed.

Pop applauded the unchanged expression. He said he could see the socialist inside me, aching to emerge.

I see the same expression every morning when I shave. I'm not a socialist. Or maybe I am. Maybe I am a close-enough socialist, whatever that may be. I think government should make an effort to take care of unfortunate people. Maybe I think that because I'm unfortunate. Or less fortunate. I don't have much in the bank, let's say, and leave it at that.

I'm not lazy. I'm willing to work. When I'm at work, I don't slack. If you know someone who might have a job for me, please let me know.

For women, I've always been the spare tire in the trunk of the car. I'm not particularly handsome, but I'm adequate enough that a woman might think, "Sure, why not?

If all else fails, there's him." I'm fine with that. As the philosopher said, "Beauty is a short-lived tyranny."

I remember asking a girl named Elaine to the senior prom. She took a week to say yes. When we got to the prom, she stared across the gym floor at the actual male person who stirred her heart, a future bond trader named Rhino.

I finally said, "Do you want me to go get him? Rhino?"

Elaine played coy. "Who? Him? Why would I want you to do that?"

I could have left it alone, but I didn't. I found him out behind the gym, drinking a beer and smoking a joint, lamenting that he'd picked the only girl who wouldn't put out at this crappy prom. His date was a National Honor student named Rosalee.

"You wanna swap dates?" I asked him.

"Who you with?"

"Elaine."

He rolled his eyes. "She's flat-chested," he informed me.

"She's also ready to have sex with you."

He tossed the cigarette on the blacktop and stepped on it. "Sure. Why the fuck not?" He went back inside.

I waited a moment and then followed him in. I saw Elaine's eyes light up as he made his way over to her. Women's eyes don't light up that way for me. I'm not the type of man who inspires that sort of thing. I don't hold any resentment about it. I like being anonymous, being ignored. Being desired looks like a lot of work. Like sky-diving, I'm sure it's exciting and I'm also sure it is not something that I'd like to try out.

Having done my good deed for the day, I took off.

In the latest alumni newsletter, I saw that Rhino had been promoted in his New York brokerage firm. I don't know what happened that night between Elaine and Rhino, but that sure wasn't Elaine on his arm in the family photo next to the article, not unless Elaine grew a foot taller, had her little niblet teeth capped and a breast augmentation.

When I went to work the next night, Delores wasn't there. She was supposed to be there. She left behind a note on the back of an order pad that said she was returning to Zanesville, Ohio, and that I shouldn't follow her because nothing good could come from my following her to Zanesville. She'd double-underlined and capitalized Zanesville in each instance of its use in the note. She helpfully wrote down the address for what she said was her parents' place in Zanesville at the bottom of the note.

This is how people get in trouble, you know. Not following directions.

It was an adventure. I took the note, left the restaurant, locked the doors and shoved my key under the front mat. I could have tried to drive my car to Zanesville, but it wouldn't have made it.

I didn't have much money. I'm not very good with money. This is a problem of mine going way back. All the way back. And all the way forward, too, to the present day. Ask the raccoon, if you can find him. He didn't appreciate my situation.

I walked down to the Trailways bus station with the intention of buying a ticket to Zanesville, or maybe Cincinnati or Cleveland. I was unsure concerning the geography part of the adventure. Ohio was north. I knew that much.

At the bus station, a dude wearing a white, bellbottomed jumpsuit with "FATTU" spelled out in golden sequins sparkling on his back and sequined flames sewn into the seams from his armpits to his white ankle boots, hired me to ride shotgun with him from Florida to Ohio. I found him pacing around the bus station near the coin-operated TV sets. I'd been on my way to the ticket counter. I expected him to speak in an Elvis-inspired drawl, but he didn't. His voice was Midwestern flat. There was no musicality to it whatsoever. He spoke quickly, too. "You want to go to Ohio? Let's do this. Here's two hundred dollars." He handed me $300 in twenties. I counted it in front of him and tried to give back the extra hundred. "You keep it! You keep it! Good job! You're trustworthy. We have a circle of trust going."

I was wearing my work uniform. We were quite a pair walking out of the bus station to his waiting car, a mid-1970's Camaro painted gold, like the car in the Rockford Files, glowing under a streetlight. Or was it a Pontiac Firebird? The engine was running. I could see blue smoke rising out of the tailpipe and up into the humid air. It was the rainy season. Everything was wet—ground, trees, people, air. I flung my straw boater onto a palmetto bush growing at the edge of the lot.

Where did I leave my car? Should I have sold my car? It wasn't worth the effort to think about the car, so I didn't.

He produced an glass amber bottle of black beauties. The bottle had been around since the 1970's, like his car. Maybe he'd found it under the bucket seat. I popped a tablet, he popped four. He told me he was going to dictate his novel to me, and I was going to type it all down. He handed me an Olivetti in a brown leatherette zipped case and a roll of paper from a paper towel dispenser. "This is going to be my masterpiece. Type it all down! I'm the new Kerouac!" The speed made me feel like there were invisible live wires under my skin. I kept shouting, "Woop! Woop!" I typed the guy's masterpiece while he drove. He had an organist's keyboard built into the dash, and he played it. Bach fugues, mostly, to accompany his dictated writing. There were pipes in the doors. Every note vibrated through them.

"Her lips were pillows for my psionic mind." I remember that line. I don't remember a lot of the rest of it. Most of it was like that, though.

All the roadsigns that I'd read from my annual trips north were still there somehow (Stuckey's, See Rock City, etc.).

I typed, and the paper kept getting stuck. The ribbon was on its last legs. The paper tore, so I ripped it and tossed it in the seat behind me. I looked back at some point and there were all these curls of typed-upon paper back there.

"Is it done?" he asked me, riffing on the keyboard. "Is it done? Is it done?"

"Yes," I told him. "It's done."

"Cool," he said, and drove us off the side of a low bridge in Kentucky, bounding over rocks ten feet down before sloshing nose first into the river below.

"I should have asked for more money," I muttered as the car splashed down.

"What's that?!" he shouted.

"Never mind."

We somehow survived. I rolled down the window, climbed out of the car, swam ashore and looked back. The car was gone. So was the author.

I trudged back up to the road, drenched. I checked my front pocket and found the wad of twenties still in there, soggy. I shoved them back into my pocket. I slowly dried while I walked backward at a leisurely pace alongside the road, my thumb stuck out.

Soon enough, a man in a pink Cadillac convertible pulled over. He was wearing a seersucker suit. "You have an accident?"

"Yes. My car sank. In the river."

"Where are you headed?"

"Zanesville, Ohio."

"Small world. Get in."

He was a paper salesman from Duluth, Minnesota named Fred Jenkins. He was on his way back from a convention of paper salesmen in Cleveland, Tennessee. He had relatives in Zanesville who he meant to see on his way back to Duluth.

"Paper convention!" Fred said. "Imagine."

"Okay."

"Too much fun."

"Okay."

"Beats spending all that time on my route." He spoke of driving to print shops all around greater Duluth. His company was based in Erie, Pennsylvania.

An hour, maybe two, drifted by. We chatted amiably. We crossed the Ohio River over a buzzing bridge. After passing through Cincinnati, Fred said, "It's time to gas up." I looked over at the gas gauge and the tank was still three-quarters full.

"Okay," I said.

We pulled into the POWER PLUS truck stop. It featured an endless parking lot, asphalt as far as the eye could see, and dozens of trucks, all of them gurgling out diesel smoke in their respective spots. In the distance, I could see the restaurant. It was late in the day. The exterior walls were all composed of sheet glass that seemed to be on fire with the reflected sun. I held my hand up to my eye.

"Join me inside for waffles," Fred said, parking in a sub-parking lot dedicated to cars. "My treat."

"I need to piss," I said.

"It's around back." He gestured with his hands that I should walk all the way around the glass restaurant. "You'll see it. But don't go in the wrong door. That would be a mistake."

I hustled around the glass restaurant and found a beige cinderblock building squatting behind the restaurant. There were three doors. I picked the one with a life-sized, top-hatted gentleman in spats rendered artistically on it. The restroom was surprisingly clean. It was all white porcelain with black and white tiles on the floor, an artificial floral scent lingering in the air instead of stale urine. I relieved myself in a floor to waist-high urinal featuring a pink puck at the bottom marked with a date. I pissed the date right off that thing. Above the chrome-handled flusher at the top of the urinal was a simple black-and-white flyer: MUSEUM. NEXT DOOR. SUGGESTED DONATION $1. There was nothing on the flyer about what kind of museum it was.

I washed my hands and, after holding my hands under a weak blower, dried them on my pants, and exited the restroom. Outside the men's room, there was a door with a life-sized ballerina on it, same artist as the gentleman's room door. And next to that was a door with a simple sign. Spelled out in block letters: MUSEUM. I pushed inside.

The place felt vast, but I couldn't tell. Not for sure. It was dark, unwindowed. Directly in front of me stood a small plexiglass box, empty, on a wooden stand lit by an overhead light. I reached into my pocket and found a damp dollar bill and slipped it in there. A voice from overhead boomed, "THANK YOU." I leapt backward, startled. I reflexively looked up into the darkness. "DO NOT DEVIATE FROM THE ROUTE," the voice boomed again.

A string of subdued lights glowed on the floor like in a movie theater. I followed the trail. A light clicked on from above, illuminating a scene to the left of me. I turned to face it. Two mannequins, a man and a woman, were dressed in 1920's flapper gear. The woman held a stuffed chicken. The man held an oversized key. Dust motes floated in the beam of light. The man's straw boater, identical to the one I'd thrown away in Florida, was cocked at a rakish angle. The woman's sequined dress sparkled. The light clicked off.

I followed the string of lights to the next exhibit. The light clicked on. Two male mannequins, with the same head as the first male mannequin, stood next to each other. They were not quite holding hands. Each wore a loin cloth. A plastic goat stood in front of them. One of them held a butcher's knife. The light clicked off.

I followed the string of lights to the next exhibit. The light clicked on. Two mannequin women this time, same head as the first woman, with matching blonde bobs, dressed in matching blue coveralls and sparkless work boots, sat at a round, sheet-metal table, a can of pork and beans between them, unopened. The light clicked off.

There was nothing separating me from each of these tableaux. No velvet ropes. No barriers of any kind. I walked from one to the next for 15 minutes. I had no idea what they were supposed to be teaching me, and barely had time to take each one in before the overhead light would click off and the string of lights on the floor would urge me forward. I was unprepared for the shock of the final exhibit.

The light clicked on overhead. An actual human being sat strapped with bungee cords to a straight-backed wooden chair. He had no arms or legs. He wore a blue t-shirt, the sleeves rolled and safety-pinned in place. A pair of camouflage cargo shorts was belted to his lower body, the pants legs empty. His head and neck were painted frog green, his matted hair dyed highlighter pen green. One of his ears didn't match the other. His nose appeared to have been broken and not set properly before being allowed to heal. The whites of his eyes were jaundice yellow. "Feed me," he said, gesturing with his eyes toward a fake wood TV table a few feet away from him. There was a tablespoon next to a bowl of Cheerios on the TV table. There was no milk in evidence.

"There's no milk," I said.

"God damn it. Feed me." He opened his mouth, exposing horror show teeth.

"What's going on here?"

"I'm hungry. That's what's going on here." He opened his mouth again, wider this time. I could see the glint of the fillings in his molars from where I stood.

I gingerly walked over to the table and picked up the spoon and bowl. I felt someone grab my bicep from behind, halting me. I nearly jumped out of my skin, spilling Cheerios all over the floor. I turned around and it was Fred. "I told you not to go through the wrong door."

"He's hungry." I tried to continue over to the armless and legless man, but Fred was stronger than he looked. He held me there.

"Don't do it. Come with me. Eat some waffles."

"I'm hungry!" the man shouted. He glowered over at us. At Fred.

"Don't you do it," Fred said sternly. "Put the bowl and spoon back where you found them."

I did so, and followed Fred through the dark to the original door where I'd entered.

"Get back here!" I heard the man shouting with foaming rage. "You haven't finished! You have *not* completed the museum!"

Back outside in the late day sun, I asked Fred if we shouldn't call the police.

"Why?"

"That man."

"He's exactly where he wants to be."

"What was the point of that museum?"

"That's just like you. Always needing a point."

"You barely know me. We just met."

"I know you enough. Waffles. No more questions."

We went in the diner and ate waffles.

At 3 a.m., Fred jostled me awake. I'd fallen asleep in the passenger seat, my stomach full of waffles. "This is where you get out," he said.

I blinked. I peered around.

Fred leaned all the way over the top of me and opened my door.

"Thank you," I said, yawning.

"Don't thank me yet."

I climbed out of the land yacht and stood on the street corner. I shut the door.

Fred drove away without another word. I reached into my pockets, found the money, unmolested and now dry, and I put it back. I found the order pad in my back pocket. The note and address had washed away. I looked up at the street sign. Main Street and Pine. I peered around and saw a park, walked over to it, and passed out on a bench. I awoke a few hours later, the sun shining brightly over a sparkling river.

A police officer strolled up to me and said, "Move along, Smokey Joe."

He seemed friendly enough, so I said, "Excuse me, sir."

"Yes, Smokey Joe?" He slipped his nightstick out of his Sam Browne belt and tapped it lightly on his thigh. The gesture seemed playful, almost. He was so cheerful. I liked him right away.

"Do you know Delores Stern?"

"Do I know Delores Stern? Do I?" He rubbed his fuzzy cheeks with his free hand, ruminating the question, letting it bubble on the stovetop for a moment.

"Yes, sir."

"Only since high school." He poked me in the chest with the nightstick. "You somehow get tangled up with ol' Delores?"

"You could say that."

"I just did."

"Yes, sir."

"Since you have such obvious respect for an officer of the law, I might take you on over to Delores' place. What do you think of that?"

"You'd do that?"

"I'd do anything for a time traveller from the 1890's. If you knew me, you'd know that right away."

"Thank you, sir."

"Enough with the obsequiousness, boy. Let's go for a walk." I followed him along the river, which had a strangely savory scent about it, like a half-cooked meal. We walked over a creaking wooden foot bridge and ended up on the other side of the river, and walked a few blocks further. He gestured with the nightstick. "Thar she blows." He smiled, and I saw that one of his teeth was missing. "Misery awaits you, laddie. That's the only reason I didn't run you in for vagrancy. Delores is a far worse punishment than anything the city of Zanesville could visit upon you." He poked me with the nightstick toward a cramped, two-story, clapboard A-frame. "Go, Smokey Joe. Before I decide to give you the lighter punishment."

In retrospect, I think that maybe *I* was the punishment for her.

I heard multiple babies from multiple houses crying like an opera unaccompanied by the house band. They wailed, their voices filled with compressed fear that only the helpless and confused have. They were hungry. They were uncomfortable. They needed to be fed. They needed to be held. I nearly tripped on the crumbling front walk leading up to Delores' front steps. The front steps were crumbling, too. There was a rusted handrail on one side of the steps and two rusted out metal stumps where the other handrail had been mounted on the other side. Before I could climb the three steps and knock on her door, it swung open and Delores came out, shouting at the people inside, "My ride is here and you'll never have to see me again!"

"Delores," I said.

"Tris," she said, mocking me a bit. "Took you long enough. I'd almost given up on you."

"I came as quickly as I could."

"I can see that. You didn't even change your clothes. You look like shit." She had an Adidas workout bag slung over her shoulder. She had on a pink tube top, Daisy Dukes and gray shoes with velcro straps instead of laces. Her auburn hair was tied into a neat bun in the back. She peered around. "Where's your car?"

"It didn't make it."

"Bummer. You have any cash on you?"

"A little."

"Enough for two bus tickets?"

"Where are we going?"

"I know a guy." She took my hand and pulled me toward the sidewalk. When we got there, she turned around and bellowed, "Fuck all of you!" I studied the house. I didn't see any movement at all. She took my face into her hands, tilted it up, leaned in and kissed me. I shivered.

"Did you see that?" she shouted toward the house. "No one needs you!"

I should ask more questions. I should be more curious. I made an attempt. "Should I—?"

"Seriously. You didn't even bring a bag with you? You were in that much of a hurry?"

"Yes."

"I can work with that." She turned toward the house one last time. "Goodbye, assholes!"

We stopped at a diner and ate waffles. We stopped at Goodwill, and she picked out some clothes for me: Jeans, a plaid flannel shirt. We stopped at a drugstore and picked up some underwear and socks. The underwear was designed for hernia patients. The socks were designed for diabetes patients. We stopped at the bus station and bought two tickets for the Trailways bus, departing for Chicago the following morning.

She got us a room in the motel near the bus station. The owner, she said, owed her a favor. The room was tiny —a double bed with a stained comforter dominating most of it, a TV set on a rolling cart against the opposite wall.

She sat down on the end of the bed, her hands on her knees. I stood next to the TV set, taking in the room.

"Take off your clothes," she said. She twirled her index finger in front of her. "Get to it."

"Um."

"I'm going to see you naked at some point. Might as well be now." I looked over at the window. The curtains were drawn. "No one's going to see you. Or care. Take off your clothes."

I leaned against the wall and pulled off one shoe, then the other. Then my tight socks. I tossed them aside. "Um."

"Keep going." I unbuckled my trousers and let them drop to the floor. I stepped out of them. "You're getting to the good part. Shirt next." I unbuttoned the shirt and tossed it on top of my socks. I hesitated. I was a virgin. I was afraid of disappointing her, mainly. "T-shirt." I took off the t-shirt, pulling it over my head clumsily. I tossed it on top of the shirt. "Last but not least." I put my thumbs in the elastic waistband of my hernia shorts. "Go on." I pulled them quickly down to my ankles and then stood up hurriedly and placed both hands over my junk. "Turn around." I slowly turned around, facing the wall. "Close your eyes." I closed them as hard as I could. In a moment, I could feel her breath on my neck, her fingers stroking my shoulder blades, and then tracing their way down my spine. She pinched both ass cheeks. She leaned in and I could feel her pubic hair and her erect nipples. She nibbled on my right earlobe. "Let's get you washed up."

She led me by hand into the bathroom, and we stepped into the tub together, facing each other. "Only do what I tell you. Nothing more, nothing less." She washed me, front and back. She was thorough and gentle. She dried me with a rough towel, and then dried herself with another one. She led me by the hand to the bed, positioned me on my back in the middle of it, placing a pillow behind my head. "Comfy?"

"Yes."

"Good." She dug around in her Adidas bag and found a condom. She carefully placed it on me. She sat down next to me and kissed my lips, her hands pressing my shoulders down. She straddled me, her knees nearly in my armpits. "Let me show you something." She got up a bit. She took my hand and separated out my index and middle fingers. She placed the two fingers between her legs, and then moved the fingers around slightly. "This is my clit. Got that? Pay attention to it, but not too much."

"Okay."

"Go ahead and explore for a moment." I did. She groaned a little. "That's enough." She backed up a little and mounted me. "You can touch my breasts, but don't be too grabby, okay?" I felt her up. Her nipples went from soft and pink to hard and nearly purple. She bucked up and down. "Don't come until I tell you. I'll know if you do. And stop holding your breath. You'll come real quick if you do that." She fell into a rhythm. "There we go. There we go." She licked her lips. She took my hands off her breasts and placed them on her hips. "Here it is! Here we go!" She went faster and faster. I couldn't hold it anymore. I felt like I'd explode. "Now! Now! Now!" I came and she roared. We were both out of breath. "Whew." She rolled off me and lay next to me, breathing heavily. "How was it?"

I had no comparison for the experience. "I, um..."

"First time is always awkward. I'll bring you along."

"Thank you."

"You're welcome." She rolled onto her side, her head resting on her hand, her elbow on the mattress. She ran an index finger along my ribs. "I should have thought of this before."

"What?"

"I kept looking for the perfect man. My prince charming. But that guy doesn't exist, does he? Of course he doesn't. But this. This is doable."

"What is?"

"Find a young man. A boy really. And make your own man. Mold a likely suspect, a nice lump of clay, into what you want. That's what you are. My clay. You're gonna be my custom-made man. Aren't you?"

What could I say at that moment? "Yes."

"Now flush that condom down the toilet."

"Okay."

NEVER STOP LEARNING

I went out to get the morning paper and discovered that Liberty Entertainment LLC had claimed the naming rights to the critter who was staring at himself in the mirror in my grandparents' bathroom. According to a legal notice scotch-taped to my front door, his new name was "Doug Liberty Presents Bandit the Dancing Raccoon."

I came back inside with the newspaper and the notice and set them down on the kitchen counter. The raccoon was sitting on the counter, bleary-eyed. He'd dragged over a coffee cup. He tapped the lip of the cup and looked up at me expectantly.

"Why'd you tear up the bedroom?" I asked while pouring him half a cup. "It's hot. Don't just gulp it down."

He grasped the cup with both hands, kind of rolled back a bit, and lapped at the coffee.

I try not to let the force of an initial impression dominate the way I feel about a person. Or a raccoon. Hold on a moment, I say to myself. Let me see who you are and what you represent. Let me try to understand you. So maybe he had a bad night. Night terrors. It's a rough life being a raccoon. Maybe he felt trapped in the room.

"You have a name now." I held up the piece of paper. I pointed it out to him on the sheet.

He snatched it away from me. I think he was reading it. He certainly gave off that impression. He crumpled it into a ball and tossed it toward the kitchen garbage can. He tapped his chest. "Bubby."

"Buddy?"

"Bubby!"

"Bubby."

"Ah." He grumbled a bit. His raccoon mouth wouldn't let him form words with precision. And I couldn't speak sign language. It was a shame.

Bubby picked up his coffee again and lapped away.

The doorbell rang.

"Grand central station," I said to Bubby.

"Heh," he went, his whiskers dripping with coffee.

A tall woman wearing a pantsuit, grey with white pin-stripes, and black stiletto heels stood with her back to me, a messenger bag slung over one shoulder. She turned around, spinning on one of those heels, to face me. Her hair was a tower of afro, shaved on the sides and back, and sparkling like it was bejeweled. "My client," she said in a clipped tone. "Where is he?"

"The raccoon?"

"Of course you'd call him 'the raccoon.' That would be just like you, Mister Edgar. You are Tristram Edgar, are you not?"

"Tris," I said, extending my hand.

She looked down at my extended hand with a mixture of revulsion and contempt. "Please step out of my way. I have a court order."

"He speaks sign language. You might want to get a sign language interpreter."

She narrowed her eyes. "Are you mocking me? An officer of the court? Are you, sir?"

"I am not."

"Then you're clearly an idiot."

"I'm not gifted with great intelligence. No."

"You think I haven't done my research on you? I've been up all night reading up on you, Mister Edgar. I even read your book."

"Oh. Which one?"

"*Dick Nixon, Private Eye.*"

"Did you like it?"

"I'm not here to flatter you, Mister Edgar." She rolled her eyes, and let out a little sigh. "Okay. I thought it was pretty good. Especially having Bob Haldeman as his version of Doctor Watson and an undead JFK as his Moriarty. Setting it in the late nineteen seventies was a good call, too. You've written other books?"

"Just my senior thesis, which was published as an academic book in Norway. It wasn't fiction though."

"What's it called?"

"*Ego A-Go-Go, An Analysis of the Bubblegum Pop of the Nineteen Sixties.*"

"Never heard of it. So maybe you aren't an idiot. My client. Where is he?"

"Come this way."

She followed me into the house and closed the front door behind her. We walked into the kitchen. Bubby wasn't on the counter anymore. He was on the floor, furiously trying to open the refrigerator door.

"I'll get that for you." I opened the door for him. He looked up quizzically at the attorney, immediately losing interest in the half loaf of bread and mostly empty jar of peanut butter. "This is your attorney. Sorry, I didn't catch your name."

"LaShonda Bagby." She handed me her card.

Bubby scrambled up the barstool and onto the kitchen counter. He licked his hands and slicked back the hair on his head. "Oochy oochy," he went, and then trilled a bit from his throat.

"I can see why you think he can speak," LaShonda said.

He began signing and moving his mouth silently along with it.

LaShonda dug a phone out of her messenger bag.

"Start over," I advised Bubby.

He waited patiently for LaShonda to get the phone aimed at him properly. "Okay," she said. "Go ahead."

He signed for a while and then stopped and took a bow.

LaShonda thumb-typed on the phone for a bit and then I heard a little whoosh indicating that a message had been sent. "May I see his living arrangements?" I took her back to my grandparents' room. She shot some photos of the damage with her phone, zooming in on the hole in the bed. "These are substandard living arrangements."

"They were standard yesterday. I closed the door last night, and maybe being in an enclosed space freaked him out a bit."

"My client demands better living arrangements."

"You can take him with you if you like. He can live with *you.*"

"I'm not living with a damn raccoon," she snapped. "What do you think I am? Some kind of failed writer?"

"I'm not just a failed writer."

"Yeah, that's right. You're also a failed musician." She glanced around the master bedroom one last time. Her face softened. "You're going to have to do better, Tris."

"Yes, ma'am."

"Also, here. Sign this." She reached into her messenger bag and retrieved a legal document. I read that I would have to shoot and upload videos of 'Doug Liberty

Presents: Bandit the Dancing Raccoon' at least twice weekly. In exchange, I would receive a stipend based on total number of views. There was a space for a signature at the bottom. Doug Liberty had already signed.

So what was I supposed to do? I signed it and handed it back to her.

"Finally, you've made a good decision."

"Have I?"

"Sure." She gave me a solicitous pat on the shoulder, reached into the bag one more time and slipped me a roll of twenties. "Go get yourself and Bandit something to eat other than peanut butter. I'll show myself out."

I walked down to Eckerd Drugs to buy food and more paper towels. It wasn't so much a scenic trip as a practical journey, but I enjoyed the walk anyway. I hoped that Bubby wouldn't destroy the house while I was gone. I hoped he'd jimmy open a window and make a run for it.

I walked past the other slapped-together houses in the neighborhood. It was that kind of place. It was where people in the 1970's went in Sarasota if they didn't want to live in the suburbs but had no choice, so bought a postage stamp of land and built whatever they could afford to build on top of that. Green spots in each lawn indicated where the septic tanks were buried. Water softeners were situated next to well pumps. My teeth were permanently yellow from drinking Florida aquifer water. I suppose I could have had them bleached, but what's the point in that?

At the end of the road, a medium-sized alligator squatted, sunning himself on the sidewalk, and perhaps waiting for some small creature to wander past that wouldn't put up too much of a fight when he dragged him to the retention pond.

The retention pond was where everyone in the neighborhood had dug up fill dirt back in the day so their houses would be six inches higher than their yards to prevent home floods during the rainy season. Dig a hole in Florida and it will fill with water almost instantly. Let it sit there full of water, and birds will come by to eat the bugs that grow on the surface of the fetid water. Eventually, fish will show up. I think birds have something to do with that. Maybe they shit out fish eggs. I don't know. Once birds and fish are there, an alligator will make it his home.

Across the street from the alligator, I saw a couple of towheaded boys, maybe nine or ten years old, gathering rocks. I walked over to them. "You gonna chuck those rocks at that gator?"

"You know it, chrome dome," the shorter of the two said. He smelled like hot dogs. His face was the same color as hot dogs. He'd clearly failed, on a number of occasions, to apply sunscreen.

"Let me get out of here, first."

"You better hurry then, baldy," the other kid said. He had on an oversized, moth-eaten and sun-bleached Miley Cyrus t-shirt. Miley was naked save for a pair of brown work boots. She was riding a metal ball.

"Be careful," I said, glancing back at the boys as I hustled away.

"Buck, buck, buck!" they shouted after me, making chicken sounds.

The guy in front of me in line at the Eckerd's cashier was wearing a Freaky Frank's uniform, with unwashed tangles of hair cascading from his Freaky Frank's hat. The cashier quizzed him about Freaky Frank's. I listened in, a spectator to the conversation. For some reason, I thought it might be important for my future, in case the raccoon videos didn't work out. I thought, *Maybe I could work at Freaky Frank's. I can make sandwiches.*

Cashier: "You working today?"

Freaky Frank's guy: "No."

"Oh... um, they call you in at all hours?"

"No. I have set times." The question of why he was dressed for work kind of lingered there, unasked and unanswered.

"What kind of hours you work?"

"Thirty-two hours a week, mostly." I looked at his hands. His fingernails were all clipped down save for one of his thumbnails, which was about an inch-and-a-quarter long, chipped and yellowed.

Freaky Frank's guy was rung up, and then stood there while my stuff was being rung up. He slowly and deliberately rearranged his groceries—jerky, beer, nuts. He finally managed to get out of the way after the cashier and I stared at him long enough.

"What about you?" the cashier asked, as he finished scanning my groceries, beer and then my roll of paper towels. He shoved my non-beer stuff into two tatty plastic bags, cramming them in every which way.

Behind him was a vast array of e-cigarette liquids and the accompanying equipment. "Cherry pie e-cig liquid" caught my eye. I'd never taken up smoking, but I like cherry pie. I thought for a moment about asking for the liquid and whatever equipment it took to vape it into my body, but the thought lingered only for a moment. I looked at all that stuff and suddenly it seemed too complicated. Then I remembered that he'd asked me a question. "What? I'm sorry. What?"

"What about you? What do you do for a living?"

"Oh." I thought about it for a moment. "I guess I make videos now."

"Oh yeah? Anything I've seen?"

"Made a video of a dancing raccoon last night."

"Oh, you're *that* guy? That's hilarious! I've watched that like ten times already. You gonna make more of that raccoon?"

"Yes. I am contractually obligated."

"Cool beans. Are you part of the Eckerd Drug Club?"

I shook my head.

"No? You can sign up for the club online. You should think about it. Mention that I sent you. Ramon from store one-fifty-seven. You can find me using the drag-down menu on the third screen of the sign-up page. I get a year-end bonus based on the number of people I get to sign up for the Eckerd Drug Club. You'll get fifteen percent off your next purchase of twenty-five dollars or more. Plus they'll email you coupons for things you buy frequently. Would you do that for me? Would you sign up for the club?"

"Sure."

"Thanks, man. That'll be nineteen ninety-five."

On the way home, I was careful to look for the alligator. And the kids. I didn't want to get pelted with rocks. I saw the gator outside the front door of a sloppily put together home, its jaws wide open, hissing. A few feet to the left, I saw the two kids through the front window. They were jumping up and down on the couch. They saw me watching them, and made chicken wings out of their arms. They continued jumping up and down and flapping their improvised wings. I hurried along.

I unlocked the front door, my three plastic Eckerd's bags in various states of disrepair, threatening to vomit up the groceries. "Bubby! Hey, Bubby!"

He came around the corner from the kitchen, and then looked a bit disappointed that it was me and not the tall, attractive attorney. "Bubby," he went. "Bubby."

"You want some baloney? American cheese? I got Wonder white and yellow mustard. Fritos? Beer? Bet you're hungry."

He climbed up on the counter and rubbed his hands together. All three bags fell apart into thin shreds as soon as I set them down. He dug through the groceries and found the baloney. He peeled up the back of the container and delicately removed a single slice. He gingerly removed the red plastic ring from around the baloney slice, rolled the slice into a tube and gobbled it down.

"Hold on. Do that again." I pulled my phone out of my pocket.

He put the lid back on the baloney container and waited for me to get the phone aimed at him. Once I did, he repeated the process, and then licked his fingers. "Ba-oh-knee!" he went. He swayed from side-to-side making jazz hands, and then keeled over and belched.

I uploaded the resulting video and named it, "Doug Liberty Presents: Bandit the Dancing Raccoon... eats baloney!!!" #hangry #doalittledance

I wondered what my recently dead grandfather would think of all this. I wasn't exploiting the working class exactly. I was exploiting a talking, dancing raccoon. Or rather, I was participating in exploiting a talking raccoon. I think the raccoon was participating, too, so was it really exploitation?

Exercise: Define "exploitation."

Discuss.

TEACH OTHERS WHAT YOU KNOW

Here's something you shouldn't mention if you're apply-
ing for a minimum wage job stocking shelves at your local
Buy and Bye superstore: I have a BA in Philosophy. I
guarantee you the BA in Philosophy has no pull with the
person hiring you. It has the opposite effect.

Should I come up with a thesis statement for this raccoon recollection? No, I shouldn't. But I have thesis
statements. Several. I'm not going to share them with you
as a thesis statement in bold letters. That would be telling,
and I don't tell.

I show. I make show.

Let's show me coming home from work as a young
man. I am home at my grandparents' house, the house
where I was raised by my grandparents. This is the house
that I later occupied with my raccoon companion.

My grandparents, I came to understand, had ended up
being roommates. I had to say hello to each of them when
I arrived home in the early morning, hazy from lack of
sleep, but unable to sleep thanks to a liberal application of
coffee down my throat and transiting my guts, until eventually the caffeine accumulated in my shriveled brain,
which spun and spun in a decidedly unsocialist manner.
Ambition was percolating. During my non-sleep I was
writing crazy diatribes to book publishers, sending them
each a Xerox copy of my book-length senior thesis. One
would eventually decide to publish the book, I knew deep
down in my gutty guts. After that, I would be a wandering
fool, pockets stuffed full of post-publication cash. Rich! A
king!

What can I say about the too-much time I spent in college—those four wasted years? I spent too much time in college. There. I said it.

I wrote two manuscripts at two different times in my life. One, a senior thesis. The other, a few years later, a detective novel. They both became books. I have royalty checks that regularly arrive at my home of record, my grandparents' house, that prove that they're both still in print. Someone's reading the things. It's gratifying. The royalty check plus ten dollars equals a sack of groceries.

"Hello, Pop." Grains of dried goop crumbled out of the corners of both of my eyes. I knuckle-rubbed them across my gray cheeks.

He grunted. He looked up from *The Daily Worker*, which was a weekly publication he received in the mail from the Communist Party of the USA. It earned him a monthly visit from an FBI agent.

The FBI agent's name was Hank. Sometimes he sat across the street from our home in a Chevy Cavalier, the window of his off-white fleet vehicle rolled down, his fingers drumming along with the AM radio in the car. *Sky rockets in flight. Afternoon delight.*

Hank was not in evidence that morning. This was maybe a week before I ran off in pursuit of ex-wife number one: Delores.

I helped myself to a cup of coffee and said hello to Matka. She peered over the top of the Sarasota *Sun-Intelligencer* at me. I sipped my coffee and hallucinated that the banana magnet on the fridge was having gastric distress. Its banana tummy was rumbling. "Shhh," I went at the banana magnet. If it made too much noise, my grandparents would hear it and know that I was crazy. I put down my coffee and slipped past the fridge and now farting magnet. "Quiet!" I whisper-hissed at it. "You'll get me in trouble."

"What's that, dear?" Matka asked.

"Nothing! No, not a thing. I'm fine. I'm dandy. What could possibly be wrong?"

I walked out to the mailbox, opened it up, and found an acceptance letter from a small academic publisher in Norway. Norway! How exciting.

I brought the letter and accompanying contract inside the house and signed it all up with a Flair pen that my grandfather had left behind after using it to do the Communist League of Youth Crossword Puzzle. Three down: "History repeats itself, first as tragedy, second as..." a five-letter word starting with an F.

The banana magnet, having gotten its farting out of its system, now offered up some sterling advice: "You should have taken that to a lawyer before you signed it."

"What do you know? You're a banana magnet." This is a classic *ad hominem* attack, of course. Here I was: Guilty of a logical fallacy. I apologized to the magnet. "I'm sorry, Mister Banana Magnet."

"Are you gender norming me now?" it asked. "Is that what's happening? First you denounce me in a most fascistic manner, and now you're saying that I have a banana penis."

"I said no such thing."

"You implied it. Your whole generation. Your entire age cohort. You didn't experience Vietnam and the peace movement, and you're bound to repeat the mistakes made back then. Look into the future."

"The future?"

"It's hidden in nickel-plated sinks, but only if you shine them up."

"What's that, dear?" Matka shouted from the next room.

"I'm reading!" Pop shouted back.

"I'm going to polish the kitchen sink," I said. "Do we have any Sheila Shine?"

"What's Sheila Shine?" Matka asked.

"If you have to ask, we don't have it," Pop said.

"What?" Matka wailed.

"If you have to—" He snorted. "Never mind."

"What am I asking?" Matka asked. "What the hell is going on in this house? Why do we need Sheila Shine?"

I knelt down and opened the door under the sink. There was a can that I'd obviously taken from work. "Ah, hah! I win! I'm going to scrub the sink!"

"The sink is fine, honey. You don't need to scrub it."

"Wrong! The sink is not shiny enough."

"I'm going to go sit on the porcelain throne for a while," Pop announced, snapping *The Daily Worker* to the next page. "Maybe there's some peace and quiet to be had back there."

"Yes! The struggle!" I shook the can and then sprayed down the sink. I rubbed it with a paper towel.

"Keep going. You're close," the banana magnet said.

"I can see it."

"See what?" Matka asked. She was standing right next to me. Her circus skills allowed her to tiptoe silently. She may have performed a silent backflip on the way. Who knows?

"Um. I'm not crazy."

"Of course not."

"I'm getting a good shine on this sink."

"It's not necessary."

"I think it is. I can see." A little picture appeared in there, like Bloody Mary when you rub your closed eyes raw and then open them suddenly while standing in front of a mirror. What was this future? What did it have to do with Vietnam and the peace movement and my generation, whatever that generation happened to be? I think I'm a Generation Xer. Maybe.

Yes.

No.

Yes: That one.

I saw my face, but it wasn't my face. It was like me, but old.

"What's this?" Matka asked.

"The future. But it's unclear."

"You should take this to a lawyer."

I turned around and realized she was reading the Norwegian book contract. "That's what the banana magnet said."

She gave me a sad, sympathetic look. "You need to quit that job. Take a month off."

Job? What was she talking about? The future was at stake. Oh, right. I had a job at an 1890's themed restaurant that was killing me. Right. Got it. "Yes, maybe I need to do that. With my book money."

"They're sending you three hundred dollars for your advance. You won't get very far on that."

"Oh."

"And the banana magnet can't talk, honey."

"Right, right." I peered past her. The magnet had lost its anthropomorphic qualities. I looked down into the shined sink and saw only my haggard reflection staring back up at me. "I should sleep."

"Stay right here." She hurried out of the room, went back to the master bathroom.

"I'm in here!" Pop shouted.

"I'll only be a minute!" Matka shouted back at him. She returned with a couple of bottles of pills. In one bottle, there were blue pills with tiny hearts cut in the middle of them. I took one.

"Take two, honey."

I took a second one. "What about the other?"

"Take two."

There were white pills with numbers on them. I took two. I drank out of the tap. I stumbled off to bed.

That was the day that I dreamt that Richard Nixon was a private detective. It was a vast, gloomy, orange-hued dream full of co-conspirators. They were all there. All of them. All the disgraced President's men. Even Kissinger was there, droning on and on. He had a fez on, and a smoking jacket. He'd written Dick Nixon a secret note that required a lemon wedge to be squeezed over it in order to read it. G. Gordon Liddy was on top of a burning oil derrick shouting, "Top of the world, Ma!" John Ehrlichman drove a getaway car. "Look at us, Dick! We've got the band back together. We're making music with our gats. Disco, my sweet fat ass!"

I awoke and wrote it all down in a waterlogged school notebook that was half-full of Kant. I didn't understand Kant. I don't think Kant understood Kant. What is the thing-in-itself? What does it mean to know the unknowable, that thing that our senses and language cannot fully comprehend or describe? I wrote for an hour, maybe two, scribbling manically with a Bic pen. I gave up writing when I smelled goulash. I tossed the notebook into a drawer, where it remained until my first divorce brought me home to Sarasota.

I came home to my grandparents' house after my divorce, following a 36-hour bus ride, riding the Trailways bus, tears in my eyes, inconsolable. The one good thing about crying like a child was that no one, not a soul, sat in the seat next to me during the entire ride. The bad thing was that a series of bus drivers shouted at me to shut the fuck up. One driver stopped the bus, pulled me out of my seat, took me out onto melty blacktop, I don't even know where, and smacked me with his open hand. "Bitch slap for a little bitch!" a pregnant teenaged girl shouted through the window. I wept a gallon of tears.

We'd been married in Chicago, but divorced in Nevada. She'd found someone else, my Delores. She declared him perfect. "You're still a work in progress," she told me, directly after telling me she'd slept with perfection. "You still need time in the oven. Or maybe you're out of the oven, but you need to cool on a window sill. Some powdered sugar on top. Something, something." She told me to get on the bus with her, we were going to Vegas. We ended up in Reno instead, and agreed to a no-fault divorce from a judge who wore a top hat. I asked him about the hat, and he told me that he was bringing elegance back to the law.

After the divorce was good and legal, Delores chased me to the bus station and bought me a ticket back to Florida. "Return to your point of origin," she said. "Go be with your people. Eat an orange. Sleep on the beach. Listen to Jimmy Buffet sing about rum and having fun." As the bus pulled away, I saw a man sidle up to her, take her hand, and then kiss her. I watched them walk away from the bus station together. I was cuckolded like nobody's business. In retrospect, they were a nice looking couple. Age appropriate, unlike her and me. Me and her.

I walked from the bus station to my grandparents' house. Matka answered the door and embraced me. We sat in the living room on the couch, while Pop sat in his reading chair attempting to ignore me. He was upset by something.

I told my story to Matka, who asked, "You're married?"

"Not anymore. Not according to the state of Nevada."

"Nevada," Pop muttered with a snort, licking a thumb and flipping to the next page of *Mother Jones*.

"But you *were* married?"

"Yes, Matka."

"And I didn't even get to see the wedding."

"Or the divorce." I burst into dreadful tears. Agonized tears. Boo-hoo-hoo. Heaving chest and all. My chest and gut ached from all the crying and heaving. I bet it's a quality workout, crying and heaving, like the AbCruncher as seen on TV.

Pop had to leave the room. He was disgusted with me, but not because I wept. It was because I was wearing a t-shirt with a corporate logo on the front of it (APPLE COMPUTER). I was also wearing a pair of pristine Air Jordans that I'd bought in a Goodwill store on the South-side of Chicago on Western Avenue. They were both signs that I'd given in to the grotesque will of the 13 families that secretly ran America, the enemies of the proletariat.

Matka was pleased to see me, but distressed that I was distressed. She offered to make me soup. Soup cures all ills, especially when it is made with bones. She left and came back a half-hour later. She brought home something from the butcher. It looked like a human femur when she pulled it out of the brown paper bag. "Shhh!" she went conspiratorially. "It is from Publix!"

Like I'd know what a human femur looks like.

She told me to go to my room. To sleep. To be still. "Disappear inside yourself," Matka advised. "Like you did when your parents died."

"Like when I accidentally killed my parents. And my sister."

"And your brother. Go! You'll know when to come back out here. Your hunger will tell you."

I hadn't eaten since the road. Certainly not since hitting the state line of Florida. I wasn't hungry. I did as I was told. I went to my room. I sat on my bed. I opened a drawer. I found the old notebook, untouched.

Ugh. *Kant.*

Wait.

What's this?

When did I write this?

Huh.

I dug around in my closet. Trapped under a pile of old textbooks that I never bothered to cash in, I found the Apple PowerBook Duo that I'd bought from the campus pot dealer during my freshman year of college. I plugged the old laptop into the wall socket next to my twin bed and it chimed to life. I sat crosslegged on my bed, the computer on top of the bed pillow on my lap, my back leaning against the wall.

All of my old papers were still scattered around the desktop and the hard drive. I opened one up with Claris Works and attempted to read it. I had no idea what I was talking about. "Philosophy is hard!" I think I said out loud.

Then I opened up a new file, dragged over the stained old notebook, and typed what I'd written years before into it. Hours may have gone by. I read and reread what I'd typed, and then started working on the prose, revising. Editing. Expanding. I saved the file as "Dick_Nixon_Private_Eye.cwk."

I was hungry, and the soup smelled like heaven.

I found my grandmother in the kitchen, sipping some broth out of a china cup with tiny pink flowers painted along the brim. The cup came from the old country, wherever that was. "Did you sleep?"

"No. I found my old computer from college and typed some stuff from an old notebook into it."

"You and your schoolwork." She smiled, not unkindly. She gestured at the soup. "It's almost ready."

"Ready enough?" I picked up the ladle and a heavy ceramic bowl.

"Ready enough."

I ladled some soup into the bowl, found a soup spoon in the silverware drawer and took it out to the dining room table. My old placemat was still there. So was my grandfather, slurping at the head of the table.

"Do me a favor," Pop said.

"Anything." I set my bowl down on my placemat, and took my seat. My old ass-groove was still in evidence.

"Burn that stupid t-shirt. And buy some workingman's shoes. I'll give you the money."

"I'll pay you back when I get a job."

"Don't get a job. Sit for a while. You've enriched the ruling class enough for the time being."

"Maybe I'll write a book."

Pop perked up. "Yeah? What about?"

"Nixon."

"It's about time someone wrote a book about Nixon."

"Everyone's written a book about Nixon."

"But not from the worker's dialectic."

"How did the Soviets feel about him?"

"They were kinder than Americans were. Sometimes, I don't understand the Party."

We spooned soup into our mouths. It was mildly seasoned, composed of bone broth and root vegetables. It was pleasant, like being home again was pleasant.

My grandmother sat at her place at the table and watched us both eat. "Back in my performing days, I was in charge of the soup."

"We know," Pop said.

"Soup is cheap and it keeps you thin."

"We know," Pop said.

"No one wants to see a fat girl in a leotard," Matka said.

"You'd be surprised," I said.

"Where were you all this time?" Matka asked.

"Chicago, mostly. I worked at Buy and Bye at night, unloading the merchandise and stocking shelves. We lived in a two-flat with four other couples in Canaryville on the Southside. It was all right." I put down my spoon, as emotion percolated up, and I fought off my tears. "I've got to go write that book now. So I don't think about her."

Matka glided over and kissed me on top of my head. "Go. I'll clean up."

"Thank you."

"Thank you for coming home. I worried about you. Disappearing like that. Don't do that again."

"I won't," I lied.

"And take a shower. You stink."

A few months later, I finished my manuscript. I printed it off and mailed it to a mom-and-pop publisher I found online.

Branchés Books was based in Brooklyn. According to the "about" page, Branchés Books was created after Timothy Murchison had self-published a novel called, *Fuck You, You Fucking Fuck*. It was celebrated, according to the chorus of blurbs by obscure authors shared on the website, as "a triumph of dirty realism." Timothy and his wife Irene also published bar guides for dive bars in the Pearl District, Wicker Park, Williamsburg, Little Five Points and East Austin. They also published book-length invectives by low-level academics condemning the ruling classes. I figured a detective novel about Richard Nixon prowling the mean streets of San Clemente would be right up their alley.

I found a job via the classifieds of the Sarasota *Sun-Intelligencer* at a tavern in Gulf Gate as a line cook, mostly deep-frying various frozen food items and dumping the crispy remains into paper-lined baskets. French fries. Onion rings. Chicken strips. Pork tenderloins. I carried with me the savory scent of beef tallow.

I became infatuated with a barmaid, and she rejected me.

I saved up some money. I had no expenses. I rode a bicycle that I bought at a police auction back and forth to work. It was a ten-speed that someone had deliberately turned into a one-speed.

Showering washed one layer of sweat and grease off so that another would take its place.

Hank the FBI agent drove me to work one day. It was the rainy season, and my makeshift garbage bag poncho had fallen apart.

Hank said, as he piloted the Chevy Cavalier across rain-slicked asphalt, "You look like shit."

"Thanks."

"I have to ask this."

"Yes."

"Because I've been observing you since you were a child."

"Yes."

"What the fuck are you doing with your life?"

"What do you mean?"

"I mean, you could be an academic right now. You could have gone to Princeton or Yale on a full-ride. You could be teaching college and writing cockamamie garbage that other academics would teach. Writing weird crap about... who's that guy? Kant? Instead, you're a fry cook."

"So?"

"'So?' Is that all you have to say for yourself?"

"Yup. That's about it."

He stopped in the alley behind the tavern. "Don't forget to pull your bicycle out of the trunk." The trunk was half-shut over the top of the bike, and secured shut with a set of government-issued jumper cables.

"Thanks for the ride."

"On behalf of your federal government, thank you for not becoming a communist like your grandfather."

"You're welcome."

"And do something with your life."

"Sure."

"Writing a shitty detective novel about Richard Nixon isn't doing something with your life, by the way."

"Okay." I looked over at him. "Wait. It was shitty?"

"It had its moments. But yeah. It wasn't great."

"Oh."

"But that Murchison character and his wife are going to print it up anyway. They're going to offer you $600 for the advance."

"That's good news."

"You'd make more than that at your job in a week if you'd work a couple of extra shifts like the assistant manager keeps asking you to do."

"I'm fine."

"You're not fine. Get it together, Tris. I mean it."

"I'll try."

I got out of the car, went around the back, pulled my bicycle out of the trunk, tossed the jumper cables in the spare tire well, slammed the trunk shut, and waved good-bye. The tires chirped as Hank pulled away.

Six hundred dollars. Pretty good, I thought.

The promised $600 became $300, because Murchison gave me half up front, and promised me the other half after "delivery of the manuscript." We spoke on the phone:

"But you have the whole manuscript."

"I have your version of the manuscript. I will edit it with you."

"Edit it? Are there typos?"

"We shall turn this promising blob into a great American novel."

"Oh. Do you really need me for that?"

"What do you mean?"

"I mean, you clearly have an intent for this thing. Wouldn't my intent get in the way of your intent?"

"It is *your* work. Aren't you interested in the final result?"

"You have the final result. It's there in your hands."

"This is raw cookie dough. It has no chocolate chips. No walnuts. No raisins."

"Who puts raisins in cookies?"

"A lot of people put raisins in cookies, amigo. Plenty of people do."

"I don't."

"Not even oatmeal cookies? Come now."

"I don't like oatmeal cookies. And you were describing chocolate chip cookies."

"Maybe I was. Maybe I wasn't."

"You explicitly mentioned chocolate chips. And walnuts." I made a mental note to ask Matka to make me chocolate chip cookies. No raisins. Not that she ever made any with raisins.

"Think of me as Maxwell Perkins. Without Maxwell Perkins, there would be no *Look Homeward, Angel*. No *Farewell to Arms*. No *Tender is the Night*."

"Um. I wrote a silly book about a failed president becoming a private detective."

His voice took on an angry tone. "It is so much *more* than that! It is a *denunciation* of the American system! My God, man! You have no idea of the *absolute gravity* of your work."

"Uh."

"We need to work on your biography. It needs to be more compelling."

"Why?"

"Let's say, 'A fatherless alcoholic, he toils in the backwaters of American capitalism, flying under the radar as a fry cook in a seedy dive bar in a nameless town in the cracker country of Florida.'"

"Sarasota has a name. It's Sarasota."

"Let's say, 'He graduated magna cum laude from Florida's most prestigious college where he went on full scholarship.'"

"My grandfather paid. And New College doesn't give out grades. They don't believe in it."

"Truth is stretchy. Remember that. No one will question this bio."

"Also, I'm not an alcoholic." Not at that point anyway. Given time, though, I worked up to alcoholism.

"Nobody knows that."

"I know that."

"Nobody knows you. They'll have to accept our word that you're a hopeless alcoholic because your family died tragically in an automobile crash."

"How do you know that?"

"Also, you need to get a website together. Irene, my lovely wife, can do that for you. I need a photo of you, unshaven with a cigarette in your mouth and a can of Pabst

Blue Ribbon in your hand. You must look depressed. Do not smile for the photo!"

"How did you know about my family?"

"I have ways of knowing things that go beyond what your feeble mind can comprehend."

"Try me."

"Never mind how I know things. It will all go into your bio. We're doing an initial print run of four thousand copies. It will sell out in a matter of weeks, or possibly days. You will need to go on a book tour. Irene will set it up. You'll hit all the hot spots. People are wild about independent press books these days. You'll see."

A year later, after Murchison had cut my book down by about a third and had added in typos and grammatical errors, he declared the book a masterpiece that would not be a masterpiece without him. I received a galley in the mail, and wrote him a long email pointing out all the typos and grammatical errors. Also, the cover was ugly, and my name was misspelled on the front and back covers: Troy Edger.

"THE BOOK IS AT THE PRINTERS," he replied. "IT IS TO LATE TO MAKE CHANGES; IT IS PERFECT AS IS."

I wrote him back, "What about my name?"

"Your nomme du plume, which is NOT A MISTAKE reflects your new status at the leading edge of post-modern literary historiography."

"Can I have the rest of my advance now?"

He didn't respond to that email. But Matka took an interest in the $300. She asked me about it, and I told her that he'd changed my name for the book and hadn't given me the rest of my advance. While I was at work, she called up the Branchés Books phone number, and got Irene on the phone. Irene promised to cut a check and change my name on the cover. She also told Matka that Timothy had a cousin who worked at the New York Port Authority who had access to the FBI national database.

When I got home from work, I checked my email and found an angry missive from Timothy in there:

"HOW DARE YOU SICK YOU'RE GRANDMOTHER ON MY WIFE WHO IS GOING THROUGH A COM-PLICATED ILLNESS AND NOW YOU'VE COST US THE COST OF REPRINTING YOUR BOOK WHICH YOU AGREED TO FULLY. I HOPE YOUR HAPPY, YOU FUCKING FUCKER. BURN IN HELL."

A check for the $300 arrived in an envelope a few days later, signed by Irene, along with a letter apologizing for the delay and a schedule of my book readings around the country, and a list of addresses where other Branchés Books writers lived. "Ask them if you can crash on their couches!" Irene wrote, along with a hand-drawn smiley face.

They'd even found a semi-famous writer, Lloyd Waggoner, to blurb it: "Reading this book is the rough equivalent of plunging to a fiery death in a cactus-laden canyon, which is the best and only way for a true man to die."

Pop lent me his car, a 1972 Dodge Dart Swinger that hadn't left the garage since his days at the National Council on Weights and Measures. Since his retirement, he preferred to stay indoors, ordering groceries from a Serbian grocer who had a poster of Marshall Tito displayed prominently on the wall. Matka drove on occasion, mostly to visit with old circus friends or to make secret visits to

Publix. Her car, a Ford Ranchero, was more functional than Pop's, but she wasn't willing to part with it, and I didn't ask her for the keys.

The first stop on my tour was in Brooklyn, the WhyNot Bookstore. I stayed with Duster Mails, whose book, *My Search for Sporty Spice*, was, according to the back cover blurb, "a quirky and compelling riff on the nature of the desire to have anonymous sex with a celebrity." He lived in a loft in a former industrial building. Everything looked expensive.

"Timothy tells me that I'm a genius," Duster said.

"Should I take my shoes off?"

"Yes." He had a neatly trimmed Van Dyke that he stroked continually. "I'm not used to having guests. At least not male guests. Ha, ha!"

"Nice place."

"My parents left me a sizable trust fund. That made it possible for me to attend the Iowa Writers Workshop. Did you go to Iowa? I wrote my book at Yaddo after I received a grant from the National Endowment for the Arts."

"Oh. Are they dead? Your parents?"

"My God, man. What would give you that idea?" He showed me around his place. "Natural bamboo flooring. Granite countertops. The coffee table is made of poured concrete. There's the bathroom you'll use. Here's the couch. I have to go to a cocktail party now. Don't wait up. Don't touch anything. I'll know if you touch anything."

"What if I get thirsty?"

"I left a plastic cup for you on the bathroom sink. I locked the liquor cabinet."

He returned in the middle of the night with a giggling woman on his arm. "Shh!" he went. "That other writer is here. The alcoholic from a white trash family. Don't wake him up. He may stab us."

"Timothy and Irene throw the best cocktail parties, don't they?"

"They know how to cultivate talent."

The next evening, I read first at the tiny bookstore. I thought I'd picked out a good chapter to read, but no one seemed interested. They drank coffees, smoked clove cigarettes and conversed as if I wasn't there. The only one paying attention was Timothy, who'd shook my hand limply about five minutes before I went up to read. He sat next to Duster in the back, ten feet away from the podium, glowering at me. When one of the lines got a chortle out of a few people, he turned to Duster and said loudly enough for me to hear, "I wrote that line. Not *him*."

Duster nodded primly.

I finished and received a quick burst of applause that sounded like a flock of pigeons had been startled into flight.

Timothy introduced Duster, and the tiny crowd cheered.

They hung on every word he read, laughing their lungs out when he looked up from the book. They weren't belly laughs, exactly. The laughs came from higher. Closer to the collarbone.

I snuck out, backtracked my way to Duster's apartment, and found my grandmother's car in the underground garage. I'd already tossed my backpack into it. I drove out of New York to Boston. Then from Boston to Atlanta. Then from Atlanta to Austin, Texas. Then from Austin,

Texas to San Francisco. Then from San Francisco to Portland, Oregon.

In Portland, I stayed with a writer named Gypsy Diamond who'd written a memoir about her life as a stripper called, *Sex and Drugs and Taking My Clothes Off for Emotionally Damaged Men.* She was covered over in tattoos and piercings. Her hair was a combination of violet and black. I read, "I'M UP HERE" tattooed in tiny letters in a forehead crease. She handed me a copy of her book, and then stood over me and occasionally paced while I read it. The book had extra large print, and even then it was only about 100 pages long. Took me about an hour to finish.

"So? So? What do you think? Huh?"

"It made me sad."

"Good, good!"

"Are you going to come and see me read tonight? The last couple of stops, we've only had a dozen or so people. It's kind of depressing." Duster stayed in four-star hotels. I stayed with whatever local author Branchés Books had in the area. Most of them had written the hipster bar guides and were excited to have an authentic alcoholic staying with them.

"I can't. I have to work tonight."

"Oh."

"I'm still stripping."

"Oh."

"Aren't you going to ask me where?"

"No."

"You don't want to come to my club? Not interested?"

"Not after reading your book."

"Fine. Be that way." She left, slamming the front door behind her.

Duster and I read our usual passages out of our respective books. By this time, I'd managed to slow down my delivery after several audience members confronted me in Atlanta and also in Austin about sounding like a carnival barker or an auctioneer.

After the reading, I signed a couple of copies for the two people who wandered up to my table. Duster went on a bookstore tour with the staff, who fawned over him. It was a vast bookstore taking up the entirety of an old high school.

I wandered around. There was a poorly lit bar in the old faculty lounge. I sat down in a school chair with a wooden seat and seat back, and a desk attached. I'm not a large man, but if I'd had any more circumference, I wouldn't have fit. A waitress wearing a Portland Books t-shirt brought over a menu. On the front were mixed drinks that were popular in the 1960's and 1970's. Whiskey sour. Manhattan. Tom Collins. On the back were menu items that featured cow hearts, goat testicles, chicken liver, tripe, pig skin, bone marrow, and so on. I chose the lamb sweetbread shish-kabob and a Pink Squirrel. The waitress squinted at me and declared me disgusting.

The food and drink, as it turned out, were disgusting.

I left the bookstore and walked around Portland. It was rainy. It took me a while to realize that everyone I saw was white, which creeped me out. Everyone dressed as if they were poor. Some of them were actually poor.

I threw up most of the boozy pink milkshake and lamb's charcoaled thymus gland in a thick brownish splatter onto a cobblestoned street.

I went back to Gypsy Diamond's apartment and fell asleep on her couch.

She woke me up the next morning with a shake of the shoulder. "How'd it go?"

"Dozen or so people. Signed a couple of books."

"You have the worst breath ever."

"I brushed last night, but I can't seem to get that shish-kabob out of my mouth."

"You didn't tell me that you eat meat."

"I eat meat."

"Get out of my house."

I drove across the country, sleeping in the back seat of the Dart at rest stops along the way. Occasionally, a highway patrolman would knock on the window and tell me that sleeping wasn't allowed at this rest stop, and that I should move along.

I moved along.

The Dart broke down in Iowa. The wiring harness caught fire. Two of the six cylinders had frozen. No oil in the crankcase. All the gaskets had rotted, along with all four tires.

I called my grandparents with the news.

"What do you want to do?" Matka asked.

"I'll stay here for a while," I told her.

"Why?"

"Why not?"

"So this is it. You've flown the coop forever again."

"Maybe it's about time."

"Maybe. I'll put your grandfather on."

Pop asked if I needed anything.

"No."

"Okay then." He hung up.

Bubby and I sat on the couch eating Fritos out of the bag and drinking Red, White and Blue beer out of the bottle. We didn't have cable, so the only channel we got was Channel 42, Southwest Florida's Independent Television Station.

Bubby signaled to me when he wanted a sip. I'd tip the beer near his mouth and he'd chug for a second or two.

The Guy Morton Show was on. Women with babies and toddlers sat in a row on the set awaiting the results of paternity tests, while the studio audience chanted "Guy! Guy! Guy! Guy!" Everyone on the show, including the babies and toddlers, appeared to be drunk.

I was certainly getting there. So was Bubby.

Doug Liberty owned the station, like he owned a lot of things in Sarasota. His main source of cash, as far as I could tell, was his car dealership, Doug Liberty Honda/Ford/Volkswagen/Jeep/Fiat/Chrysler/Kia in downtown Sarasota. One of his commercials popped on. In this one, he was dressed as Charleton Heston from *Planet of the Apes*. "It's a madhouse!" he shouted in his silver spacesuit, unshaven, his hair wild. He stepped out of a large barrel painted to look like a space capsule. A salesman dressed up like Roddy McDowell from *Planet of the Apes* jumped up and down making chimp noises. "How can you apes make a profit selling these no-mileage cars at such low-low prices?" A half-dozen more salesmen dressed as apes in suits and ties surrounded him, leaping up and down, shrieking out chimp noises. "Madhouse! Madhouse!"

"What do you want for dinner?" I asked Bubby. "Maybe we can order a pizza or something. You like pepperoni? We have plenty of beer to wash it down."

Bubby shrugged and chomped down another Frito.

Our TV watching was interrupted by a sharp knock on the door.

"I'll get it," I said needlessly to Bubby.

He signaled for another swig, so I tipped the beer into his mouth. It foamed before it went down his gullet, and then he belched.

The knock became more insistent. "Hold your horses!" I shouted. "I'm coming."

I swung open the door. A chubby gal in a floral dress squinted at me through coke-bottle glasses. Her black hair was pinched up in a tight top bun. "You look like shit," she informed me.

"Thanks."

"You are?"

"I'm Tris. But who am I really? Empirically, what can we know about ourselves, not being able to step outside of ourselves and observe our own existence?" I took another swig out of my beer bottle. "I'm talking shit 'cause I'm day drinking. Ain't day drinking fun?"

"This is reportable. I have to write out a report." She had nothing to write with. No clipboard. No writing implements whatsoever. She wasn't even carrying a purse. She had a clip-on badge fastened to the fabric covering her breasts. She unclipped it and handed it to me.

I read: PESHAWAR, S. ANTI-CRUELTY LEAGUE OF SARASOTA COUNTY, FLA. There was an unflattering faded photo of her in the middle of all that. She snatched it out of my hand and clipped it back on.

"Did you bring Johnny Law?" I asked her.

"Who?"

I nodded at the Sarasota police car parallel-parked at the curb, too close to the mailbox.

"No," she said. "I imagine he's here to keep the protesters in line."

"Protesters?"

"Look for yourself."

I walked out the front door and, sure enough, there were protesters at the end of the driveway, on the sidewalk. They had signs and everything. I saluted them with my beer, and took a deeper drink, finishing it off. Nothing but foam left in the bottom. I was ready for beer number five. "Day drinking! Ain't nothing like day drinking!"

The protesters quickly formed up like a squad of soldiers and chanted, "Hey, hey, ho, ho, the raccoon oppressor has got to go!" while waving their signs up-and-down in synch.

"Well, shit." I was a raccoon oppressor. This was a disappointing development. Boy! Talk about being assessed and defined.

The cop stepped around them and stood in-between the dozen angry people and my grandparents' house. He turned his head toward me and winked. It was that guy who I'd gone to high school with. Old whatshisname. He'd grown a mustache. Or maybe he'd had a mustache all along. Who the hell knows?

The Channel 42 Action News van pulled up in front of the cop car. The van was covered over in a graphics wrap that advertised the station. I saw a hurricane in the middle of the graphics, and beaches, and a big orange sun (or maybe it was an orange made to look like the sun), and the earnest smiling faces of anchormen and anchor-women. A spectacle of teeth and hair. A mast of sorts deployed out of the top of the van. A cameraman exited the vehicle. He carried a tripod into the middle of my yard, set it up, and snapped a camera into a slot atop it. He was wearing a headset like they do at mission control in Houston. He had on khaki trousers and a blue golf shirt. I think that's what they wear in Houston these days, too. "Cassandra!" he shouted. "I'm ready for you!"

"Hair and makeup!" I heard a woman's muffled voice call out from the van.

"Let's go. We're going live!"

"Just a sec!"

"Cassandra, huh?"

"Cassandra Liberty," the cameraman said to me.

"Like Doug Liberty."

"Duh," he went. "Where the hell have you been?"

"Chicago, mostly. Iowa before that. And Norway in the middle of that for a few months teaching college up by the northern lights, until they found out that I don't have an advanced degree. Some academics are sticklers for that. Actually, most of them are. Who's this Cassandra Liberty?"

"Cassandra was Miss Suncoast last year in the Doug Liberty Presents the Suncoast Beauty Pageant and Singing Competition."

"Okay."

"She sang, 'O Solo Mio' wearing a hot-pink swimsuit. Doug dumped his wife and married her right away."

"Ah."

"You're all caught up."

"Thanks. You want a beer?"

"Maybe later."

"I'm torn between standing here and going inside to watch it on TV."

"She'll want to interview you."

"Really?"

"And the raccoon. She'll want to get the raccoon on camera."

"I'll go ask him. I imagine Cassandra's a looker."

"You imagine right. Doug wouldn't have married her if she wasn't."

"Bubby likes the ladies. I'm sure he'll be up for it."

"I thought his name was 'Bandit.'"

"Oh. Right." The contract. "'Bandit' it is then."

I turned around. I'd left the door wide open, and S. Peshawar had taken the opportunity to go inside. It was a nice day, so it wasn't like I was letting all the air conditioning out.

I rushed into the house, closing the door behind me. I found S. Peshawar sitting in my ass groove on the couch next to Bubby. She glared angrily at me. "You've caused this raccoon to be inebriated."

"Of course I did. He can't hold the beer bottle himself. We tried that already."

"I don't think you understand."

"Understanding is not my forte."

"You could be arrested for getting this animal drunk."

"Oh, shit."

"'Oh, shit,' is right."

Bubby gesticulated at the TV. Channel 42 had interrupted its regular programming to bring us a special report from my front lawn and driveway.

"Hubba, hubba," Bubby went as the camera zoomed in on Cassandra Liberty. She had long, flowing auburn hair, a button nose and massive blue eyes, straight white teeth and an hourglass figure. Someone may have sewn her into the florescent green dress she was packed into.

"She's right out front," I told Bubby. "She wants to interview you."

"Oooo!" Bubby went. He gurgled a bit.

"Maybe you need to sober up a bit first," S. Peshawar said.

"Me or him?" I asked.

"Both of you." She took the empty out of my hand and shook it a bit.

"Plenty more in the fridge. I bought a thirty-pack this morning down at the Eckerd's on the corner."

"Thirty pack?"

"I think they call it a 'suitcase.' It was on sale. I had no choice in the matter."

Bubby left the room, drunkenly ambulating the best he could back to the master bathroom. We heard him urinating, and then the toilet flushed.

"You trained him to use the toilet?"

"He arrived with his own set of skills."

"I don't believe you."

"Suit yourself."

She took the empty into the kitchen and tossed it in the wastebasket. It clinked with its brothers.

I hummed out a few bars of Taps.

Bubby came back in. He'd combed some of his hair and was lightly scented with Vitalis.

"Looking good, my man," I told him.

He gave me the double guns and went, "Pew, pew!"

"I won't be removing the animal from the premises to-day because it appears you've formed a bond with him. However, I will come back, from time to time, to check on his welfare."

"Okeydoke."

"I'll be leaving now."

"Say hi to the nice lady out there."

She walked out the front door. I heard it open and shut. I switched my focus to the TV. The camera panned over to S. Peshawar, who immediately tensed up like she'd been poked with an electric prod. "No comment!" she shouted.

"Ma'am!" the fetching Mrs. Liberty shouted, waving her Channel 42 Action News mic at S. Peshawar like it was a light saber that hadn't been switched on. "Who are you? What's your business here?"

"No comment!"

Cassandra looked at S. Peshawar's badge. "Are you seizing Bandit in the name of the Anti-Cruelty League?"

"No comment!" S. Peshawar pushed into the dozen protesters, who stepped aside for her, and then she was gone.

I saw Bubby's attorney through the living room sliding glass door. She was climbing over the neighbor's fence in her pantsuit, waving frantically at me once she realized I saw her. She tumbled to the ground on my side of the fence, recovered and sprinted up to the door. I slid it open and she stood for a moment in the living room, panting. "Close the door."

I did as I was told. "What's up?"

She brushed herself off with her hands. "Cassandra is doing this on her own! This is *not* authorized!"

"What's not authorized?"

"Interviewing Bandit on camera. Do not let that critter be interviewed."

Bubby growled at her.

"What happened?"

"I had his sign language interpreted. From the other day? You remember? When I shot it with my phone? Anyway, it's not a good story for either one of us. He's either a lying piece of shit, or a man trapped in an animal's body."

"You want a beer?"

"I do *not* want a beer, Tris. We have to control this narrative."

My phone rang. I pulled it out of my back pocket and answered it. "Y'ello!"

"This is Cassandra Liberty, Channel 42 Action News."

"We were just talking about you. Your ears must be burning." I peered over at the TV, but they'd gone to commercial. Her husband was on the tube instead of her, wearing an Uncle Sam outfit and waving around a pair of sparklers.

"Gimme that!" LaShonda snatched the phone out of my hand.

"Excuse you." I went in the kitchen and retrieved another beer, came back in and plopped next to Bubby. I gave him the first swig.

LaShonda was whisper-hissing at Cassandra, down in a crouch. I couldn't make out what she was saying, but she was pretty animated.

A commercial came on for cashing in your 401k, buying gold, and keeping it in a safe on your property. The next one was for a lawyer who'd help you out with a lawsuit having to do with mesothelioma. Another one came on for a doctor who'd perform a non-surgical procedure that would get rid of your love handles.

"How does that work?" I asked Bubby.

"Mer-erp," Bubby went, with a shrug.

"I mean, I thought they stuck a hose in you and slurped out all the fat. Isn't that how it works? That seems surgical to me. Isn't the definition of 'surgical' cutting into the body? How would you slurp out all the fat without making a cut?"

LaShonda placed her hand over the phone and said, "They freeze it."

"Freeze it? Seriously? No kidding?"

"No kidding." She turned back around and continued her conversation with Cassandra.

"If she ever finishes up with my phone, I'll order that pizza."

Bubby gestured at his mouth, and I gave him another swig, then took one myself.

"We now return to our regular programming, already in progress," an announcer said.

The Guy Morton Show came back on. Guy's bouncer, Big Ass Ron, had to sprint into the audience and tackle a man who was threatening violence on Guy, after Guy revealed that the audience member was the father to a 14-year-old drug dealer.

"DNA tests don't lie," I said.

Bubby found it hilarious. He rolled around on the couch, holding his gut, going, "hee-hee-hee."

"Do they still call it juvie?" I asked aloud. "That seems like an antiquated term, doesn't it? Like something out of the nineteen-fifties."

"Where'd you two get another beer?" LaShonda asked, handing me back my phone.

"The fridge."

"Gimme that." She took the beer into the kitchen and poured it down the sink. "You two need to sober up. Well, maybe not Bandit."

"We want a pizza," I said.

"Fine. Later. Cassandra is going to come in here without the cameraman."

"Hot-cha." Bubby sat up on the couch and made some smacking noises with his mouth.

I sat up a little straighter.

The front door opened, and Cassandra came striding in. She was teetering on a pair of stiletto heels. She looked even better in person. She still had the microphone in her hands.

"That microphone better be off," LaShonda said. "I'm your husband's attorney, and yours, too."

"I know," Cassandra said. "Is this him? Bandit? He's adorable! He won't bite, will he?" She sat down next to him, hip-checking me aside, and he quickly climbed into her lap. "He smells just like my Dougie-Wuggie."

"Vitalis," I said.

"And you're the owner?"

"I am the roommate. No one owns, um, Bandit. Or maybe someone does. But not me. He's a rebel."

She gave off a dizzying floral scent. She crossed her shapely legs, and I think I groaned a bit.

LaShonda grabbed me by the ear and dragged me into the next room, my bedroom. "God damn, you have terrible instincts." She poked me in the chest with an index fingernail made of steel. "You are the dumbest, smart white boy I've ever met. That's the boss' wife you're leering at."

"Yeah. Shit. I know. I'm a little drunk."

"Get your act straight."

"Didn't you have a translation to show me?"

"Right." She pulled out her own phone and tapped on the screen for a moment, and then handed it to me.

I read:

I AM MAN. I FLY AIRPLANES. TRAPPED IN RACCOON. SOMEONE HELP. CALL WIFE. WIFE COME. WIFE HELP. WIFE IS FEMALE DOG. FEMALE DOG.

"I think he means 'bitch.'"

"No kidding."

I read:

MAN IN HOUSE IS STUPID. CRAZY. STUPID CRAZY MAN. HE LOCK ME IN ROOM. I WANT SEX WITH HOT BLACK WOMAN. CALL WIFE. WIFE MAKE ME MAN AGAIN. I FLY AIRPLANES.

"Did you call anyone?"

"Who am I supposed to call? The local FBI? Ask them if anyone knows the wife of a raccoon?"

"Maybe I'll call the FBI."

"The fuck you will. The FBI wants that raccoon, they can figure out where he is. They can come get him."

"I guess."

"You keep making dancing videos. But don't let him do that sign language shit on camera. You understand?"

"Yes."

"Are we good?"

"We're good."

She pulled another roll of twenties out of her messenger bag and handed it to me. "One hundred thousand views, all with a Doug Liberty ad attached to them."

"You're kidding."

"That raccoon is going to be big business. Doug Liberty has plans for him." She grabbed a handful of my shirt and pulled me close. "No sign language."

"You got it, boss lady."

ANALYZE OBJECTIVELY

I met my second ex-wife, LeeAnn Pennebaker, a photo-journalist, while flying from Norway to London to New York. By the time we arrived in New York, we'd logged 14 hours in the air together and four hours in Heathrow. We didn't shut up the entire time. I thought I knew her. I didn't know a thing.

She thought she knew me. I am unknowable.

I asked her to marry me, and she said yes.

That's not entirely true. I asked her if she was married herself. She said, "Yes. To a bum." I looked at her ring finger. There was no evidence that she'd ever worn a ring.

I said, "If you ever feel like you could use a second husband, I'm game."

That was during the layover in London. We still had plenty of flying to do.

About halfway across the Atlantic, over the rumble of cabin and jet noise, she asked if I'd been serious about marriage. She turned in her seat so that she could face me. I remained facing forward in my seat, vaguely regretting my words. She'd switched seats so she could sit next to me. Our final leg from London to Chicago was a half-empty flight, so that wasn't an issue.

LeeAnn was a thin, nervous woman with a slightly homely face. It was that face that made her irresistible to me. And her knock-knees. It's hard to explain. I'm attracted to women who muscle their way through life, who haven't been given a step up by their looks or wealth. LeeAnn was luminous with determination.

She'd died her hair to match her cornflower blue eyes. Her nails had a tiny brown face painted on each of them.

She'd explained earlier (somewhere over Europe en route to London) that the tiny faces were all rescue dogs.

She'd made me laugh several times. I'm a sucker for that.

She was estranged from her family, who lived in Glencoe, a mere a dozen or so miles away from where we settled, in Rogers Park on the Northside of Chicago. We ended up being married for a little over three years. I never met her family. I never saw a photo of them. I liked that about her, too. That we were both without a family. She'd given up hers voluntarily. I'd killed mine.

Also, there's the crushing loneliness that I occasionally acknowledge and give in to. I make the mistake of allowing a few of the people who think I'm worth knowing to think they know me during those times of loneliness. Being isolated in a foreign country, Norway, had exacerbated my usual loneliness. The darkness of winter there can crush you.

Getting to think you know me is a mistake. Ask anyone who has made the effort. I'm unknowable.

The important thing to remember about me is that I'm a welter of shitty jokes and neuroses. That's the me that I am, not the me that people want me to be.

Was I serious about marriage? "Sure," I said.

We kissed. I was so filled with ardor, I swooped in hard and chipped one of her teeth.

I followed her back to her home in Chicago, to a roomy apartment filled with boxes.

Instead of a family, she had knickknacks.

During my short unemployment phase, while I lived off a payoff from Norwegian academics who I'd lied to by omission, I dug through her things while she was away on assignment. There was no evidence of a husband, or that a husband had ever been in the apartment. I guessed, correctly, that she had moved out on him.

Never met the guy. Never saw a photo of him. When LeeAnn was done with someone, she was done with them. Except for me, as it turned out. Add that to the list of things that I liked about her. Add that to the knees, and face—the steel running through her personality.

She dominated me. I was made to be dominated.

In one box, I found cherubic figurines, all composed of ceramics. In another box, I found Disney princesses in their original boxes. In another, I found signed baseballs, all entombed in green-glass display cases mounted on wooden bases with metal plaques glued on describing the contents. "GLENALLEN HILL HOME RUN, WRIGLEY FIELD, MAY 11, 2000." In another box, I found a collection of heavy, glass ashtrays advertising hotels. "HOTEL IMPERIAL, LAKE GENEVA, WIS." In another, moist towelettes still in their original packages. In another, Zippo lighters with various engravings.

What was she doing in Norway? LeeAnn was a photojournalist who went there on a contract from a glossy periodical to take photos of people who were mesmerized by the northern lights—not the lights themselves, but the people gazing at the lights.

I had been, for most of a semester, a visiting lecturer on the philosophical underpinnings of pop music in the 1960's at the University of Honningsvåg. I'd gotten the job via the head of the philosophy department there, Professor Arnold Stang, who'd read my book *Ego A-Go-Go: An Analysis of the Bubblegum Pop of the 1960's* (based on my senior thesis) when he was a visiting lecturer at Harvard. He'd caught me between jobs. That is to say: I was working at a lunch counter in Iowa City, slinging hash, when his job offer arrived via email. He'd assumed incorrectly that I was a lecturer at the University of Iowa, and I did nothing to dissuade him of that. I'd never taught a day in my life.

Stang called me up. "May I ask you a question, please?" He asked after he offered me the job.

"It's your dime."

"Pardon?"

"Go ahead."

"This book of yours. Perhaps I have not been reading it correctly."

"I can assure you that you have not. But go ahead."

"Is it supposed to be... how to put this delicately?"

"Take a deep breath."

"It is supposed to be funny, is it not?"

"Funny ha-ha. Funny weird."

"This conversation. We could perhaps continue it here."

"Sure."

Why did I decide to stay in Iowa, post-book tour, versus going back to Florida? Crushing loneliness had something to do with it. I was doomed to be lonely, I figured, so why not stay in a place where that seemed like a lifestyle choice? Everyone in Iowa looked, to me, like they were nursing a hangover after a particularly heroic bender. I should fit right in, I figured.

Judge not.

Alcohol was involved, too. And poor judgment due to crushing loneliness and incipient alcoholism. Let's go with "mostly poor judgment." But the alcohol sure as shit didn't help. And loneliness. That's the bayonet prod in the back. Poke, poke. Do it, do it.

The reason that I'm lonely is because I killed my family in a car crash a million... a billion... years ago. I believe myself to be poison. I am poison, because I believe myself to be poison. I am the un-superman. This is my will to un-power.

I assured the venerable Stang that I could speak a bit of Norwegian. I could not. I pretended like our phone connection was shorting out and hung up on him.

The next day I skipped out on work by calling up one of my co-workers and saying, "Hey, can you take my shift today? I want to go to that new taco place and eat my weight in tacos." He understood. He took my shift.

Like my future ex-wife, I'd been keen to see the northern lights, so I had no qualms about doing a bit of lying. I bought the *EZ-Master U-Can-Do-It Learn to Speak Norwegian! 15 CD-ROM Set* from the university bookstore after flashing them an expired faculty ID card that I'd fished out of a trash can at the diner and crossing my fingers that my credit card hadn't been cut off. It hadn't. "Go Hawks," I muttered weakly to the clerk, who snapped her gum and rolled her eyes. I sprinted out of the bookstore. I returned to my apartment and realized that I had nothing to play the CD-ROMs on. My ten-year-old Macintosh LC III didn't have a CD-ROM drawer, and my boombox only had a cassette player.

At the Johnson County Fairgrounds flea market, I found a portable CD player for a reasonable price. The goddamned thing practically devoured AA batteries. I'd make it through one CD, and then have to replace the batteries. Over and over.

I learned useful phrases. *Hvordan har du det? Jeg heter Tris. Jeg liker ost. Hvor er badet, vær så snill?* And so on.

A few months later in Norway, in the middle of my lecture for a class of five bored graduate students in a vast lecture hall, all of us seated crosslegged on the lecture stage, Stang barged in and said, "This class is cancelled, and you are fired." No explanation was necessary, or desired. But it was forthcoming. The five students stood up and left without a word. "You have been, perhaps, less than honest with me?"

"I don't speak Norwegian. It's a battery-related issue."

"You also do not have a master's degree. You also have never taught a class before now. You were a dishwasher at a restaurant."

"I was a cook at a restaurant."

"It is the same."

"It is not the same. I prepared food. Occasionally, that food was delicious."

"You will be compensated for your time here."

"That's generous."

"You must you sign this document that has been written by our legal staff. You will never mention again that you taught here. We are in agreement?"

"You betcha." He handed me a Bic pen and I signed the agreement, which was written in inscrutable Norwegian. I stuck the pen in the pocket of my corduroy blazer, purchased at the Iowa City Goodwill for the express purpose of giving off the illusion of being professorial.

He handed me a check that would have paid for an entire year of grad school and, in a separate envelope, a plane ticket back to the United States. The plane ticket had me leaving the following morning, on track to meet my future second ex-wife. Like Stang, she was another human being I was destined to disappoint.

"I enjoyed your book very much. The students, they learned from your chaotic lectures. You could, perhaps, go to graduate school?"

"I don't think so."

"It is a shame."

"Life is a shame. I am a shame. Shame on me."

"Yes, Mister Edgar. Shame on you."

After our first time, as we lay side-by-side panting, covered in sweat, LeeAnn informed me that I was good at fucking. "Someone must have taught you well," she said.

"You can thank my ex-wife Delores if you run into her. She may still live in Chicago."

"Too much information. I don't want to know about your past. I don't want to know about other women."

"You brought it up."

"Now I'm un-bringing it up. Forever."

"Got it. Have I ever told you about the time my cousin Carwyn waterboarded me? This was before waterboarding was a thing. He bound and gagged me in my sleep, took me to a woodshed, strapped me to a board, placed a cloth baby diaper over my face. It's just like drowning."

"Who brings something like this up after sex? Who are you?"

"I dunno."

She thought about it for a moment. "Boy, he must have hated you. What did you do to him?"

"Nothing! I did nothing to him!"

"You must have done something."

"I am innocent."

LeeAnn insisted that I needed a real job with benefits so we could get married. She made large and infrequent lumps of cash as a stringer, but had no health insurance. She was one hospitalization away from bankruptcy. She took me to the Rogers Park Goodwill and we found a real job-getting suit, blue with charcoal pinstripes, that almost fit. I made several attempts to comb my hair in a fashion that suggested that I was a human being to be taken seriously. An application of LeeAnn's hair gel helped.

I shocked myself by finding a real job two days later via Craig's List at Prairie News Town, which sounds like a newspaper, or maybe a string of newspapers, but is neither. I wrote newsletters for corporate clients. I had to wear a tie and everything. The things we do for love.

The interview happened at a Swedish coffee shop in Andersonville. I received a complimentary cinnamon roll that I unraveled and devoured as my bookish new supervisor, Mrs. Rowlands, explained the job to me. "Philosophy. That's like psychology, isn't it?"

"Sure. Why not? Also, I've written two books, so I've got this writing stuff down."

"I saw that on your resume. You've got some icing on your chin."

"Thanks." I did nothing to rectify that situation. I was fixated on uncoiling the roll and segmenting it into bite-sized strips.

"So you'll be writing for two of our most finicky clients."

"Sure, sure."

"One of them is an, um, institution in DuPage County. The Summerlands."

"Institution?"

"It's for people who have had, um, problems."

"I see." I didn't.

"The other is the Serbian Home for the Aged. Do you speak any foreign languages?"

"Norwegian."

"I think Serbian is close to Norwegian."

"Both countries are in Europe. So in that way, you're correct."

"You're really enjoying that cinnamon roll."

"I am."

I reported to work the following morning at what used to be a supermarket in a partially abandoned strip mall in Cicero. It took me 90 minutes to get there, riding the EL on the Red Line all the way to the Loop, and then taking the Blue Line all the way to the end of the line.

I walked in through the automatic glass doors alongside a pigeon. The pigeon and I regarded each other for a moment before he flew off and landed on a cubicle divider. I peered around and saw about a half-dozen pigeons hopping from one divider to the next. There were about 30 desks and chairs under the harsh florescent glare. Three of the chairs had workers occupying them. The rest were empty.

I shucked off my winter coat. I coughed.

"Hey! Get out of the doorway!" one of my new coworkers shouted. "You're letting the heat out!"

"And the pigeons in!" another shouted.

I stepped off the rubber mat. The automatic door shut behind me.

Mrs. Rowlands hurried over. She wouldn't have looked out of place in a library, shushing the patrons. "You're here," she stated, with a bit of surprise.

We went back to HR, in the former meat department, where I filled out a number of forms, including the health insurance, and then she showed me my cubicle. There was a dusty computer with a 14-inch tube monitor, a rotary telephone with a bulky headset attached, a notepad and a Bic pen.

The florescent lights clicked off momentarily. Mrs. Rowlands waved her arms over her head and the lights clicked back on. "Motion sensor. Usually the pigeons take care of it."

Mrs. Rowlands handed me a few back issues of the newsletters I was hired to write and edit. "They don't like these. Your predecessor was a bit of a drunk. But at least you'll get the idea by flipping through them." She gave me a sheet with my points of contact for each institution on it. "Call them once you're ready. Today." Her parting words were, "Good luck. Also, you have some shaving creme stuck in your left ear."

I twirled a pinkie finger in there. "Got it?"

"No." She smiled in a way that suggested that I probably wouldn't last long. She was right. I teach people to trust their instincts about me, eventually. "You look like shit."

"Thanks."

"Just stand up and wave if you have any questions."

"And if the lights turn off."

"Yes. And if the lights turn off."

We rode the EL down to the Cook County courthouse and obtained a marriage license. We stood on the EL platform, waiting to go back home. Silent. We shivered and watched the breath cloud out of each other's mouths.

"We don't have to do this." LeeAnn was beautiful when she said that. Gorgeous.

"Okay," I said.

"Okay? Okay as in you 'don't want to do this'?"

"Okay, as in I've acknowledged what you said." Somewhere inside, I'd crossed a line. I'd stepped over a line. I saw myself as being married. I imagined myself introducing her as my wife. I saw myself as a functional person. I had a job with benefits. I had a wife. "I want to get married. To you."

"Okay," she said gloomily.

We were, neither one of us, thrilled. The next day came, and we went downtown again, back to the courthouse, and got married. A clerk took us into a little room. We recited after her. We exchanged plain gold rings.

Outside, we were jazzed on dopamine and norepinephrine. We shook in our winter coats. We hopped up and down in our winter shoes.

We went to Lou Malnati's and waited 45 minutes for a deep-dish pizza because I'd mentioned that I'd never eaten one before.

"We're married," I said, seated across from my new bride.

"Imagine that," she said.

"Never thought I'd do that again."

"Me neither. You look like shit."

"Thanks."

The pizza arrived on our table, carted over by a waitress with nicotine-stained fingers and hair that could scrub pots. She served us each our first slice on plastic plates. Utensils were required, and delivered. "Enjoy," the Sea Witch said.

I stared at the pizza on my plate. My brain went: "What is this? What have you done? What is this thing? This isn't even pizza! And who is this across the table? What are you doing? How is this happening? *What have you done?* What have you done?"

"Are you happy?" she asked, waving a fork weighed down with the pizza casserole around near her mouth.

"Ecstatic." I poked the slice with an index finger. What the hell?

I didn't drink much during my second marriage. Wait. That's clearly a lie. I drank while she was gone, to excess. The calm that I was looking for in the bottom of a glass came with being with LeeAnn. The chaos of everyday existence disappeared when I was close to her. At work, I fretted. When I came home, and she was there, I did not fret.

She did everything for me, all the things that filled me with nervous dread—the gas bill, taxes, the electric bill, doctor's appointments, doctor's bills, meal decisions, calling people on the phone to complain about bills, and so on.

"It's all about you," she said. "This is the decade of Tris." The decade of Tris was destined to last only three years.

She was homely, sure, but I loved her. Sort-of loved her. She filled a dead space inside me. She seemed to love me. She said it enough. She filled a void that had been there since my first wife jettisoned me. Delores filled a void that had been there since my family died in that car crash that I'd caused, and that I'd somehow survived.

So I *did* love Delores. I *did* love LeeAnn.

Am I lying to myself? To you? Possibly. But possibly not.

The calm lasted only as long as each day remained the same. I rode the EL to work. I called up psychiatrists at one institution and geriatric specialists at the other, interviewed them, wrote little articles that filled space in a pair of newsletters that were mostly filled with advertising for various drugs with names like Panglobin GL and Ascomil. The drugs were meant to solve problems acquired by being insane, or being old.

Each evening, I hopped on the EL again and rode home. A cheerful Canadian voice with perfect diction announced each stop. LeeAnn fixed a standard American meal—roasted chicken, meatloaf, spaghetti and meatballs. We ate and discussed our day. We sat on the couch and watched one of her competition shows on TV, which mostly involved contestants who were chefs or singers. We agreed on a person to root on. We rooted that person on and were disappointed when that person was eliminated. If I put my head in her lap, she ran her fingers through my thinning hair. We didn't spoon in bed. We didn't hold hands. We got used to watching the other person urinate. On occasion, we bathed together. We had terrific sex for about a year and a half. At some point, that faded away.

We took vacations that LeeAnn planned like they were military campaigns. Once, we rented a Honda Fit and drove up to a peninsula that jutted out into Lake Michigan, somewhere north of Milwaukee. LeeAnn had a printed-out chart with timetables on it that accounted for nearly every minute of our time there.

8:45 a.m.: Breakfast complete.

9 a.m.: Board ferry.

9:45 a.m.: Disembark ferry. Begin travel to wine tasting.

10:15 a.m.: First in line for wine tasting at vintners.

11 a.m.: Proceed to nature park.

11:15 a.m.: Ride tram through nature park. (Note: Use Nikon D1x with 55-300mm lens for photos. Don't forget to bring it!!)

It was less a vacation than some sort of Bataan death march, her angry eyes the bayonet that kept me moving from one station to the next. "Are you having fun?" she asked, over and over.

"Yes," was the mandatory answer. At the end of the ordeal, I was obligated to thank her for setting it up and paying for it.

When LeeAnn went on travel to the far reaches of the globe, I'd buy a pint of bourbon each evening she was gone and sit and look out the window of our apartment, three stories above Ashland Avenue, the lights off, the silence punctuated by loud arguments, sirens, buzzing bass speakers of passing cars and occasional gunshots. I'd roll into our pillow-top bed and stare at the ceiling, waiting for the morning alarm to tell me to go to work. I'd go into work sleepless and bleary-eyed. I'd forget my lunch and have to go to the Polish buffet in Cicero, where I'd eat my body weight in pierogi, sauerkraut and pork. I'd ride the EL back home and stop on the way back to the apartment and buy another pint of bourbon.

Sometimes, she'd be gone for a month, come home, and declare the apartment a disaster zone. "Call in the federal government! Call in FEMA!" Also: "What would you do without me? How did you survive before we met?"

I remember serving her a Cheez Whiz and Eggo sandwich upon one of her returns, as a welcome home meal. "You're an idiot." She kissed me on the forehead and mussed my thinning hair, like you would a troublesome child. "You look like shit."

"Thanks. Have I ever told you about the time my cousin Carwyn—"

"Stop it. Stop telling me stories about this cousin torturing you. I'm sick of it. I get it. You've suffered. No one cares."

If she had any friends, I never met them.

I didn't have any friends, at least not until I got fired. Then I got my old job back at Buy and Bye. Then I made a friend. Then I fucked up my marriage.

How did I get fired? I came in a bit tipsy one morning, maybe a year and a quarter into my time at the newsletter stalag. The lights in the office did not believe in me. They failed to turn on while I stumbled around.

I forgot where the men's restroom was (in the back of the former store, next to the former bakery), urinated into a fake potted palm, and passed out near the former deli when I got lost looking for my desk in the darkness.

Mrs. Rowlands nudged me awake with the toe of her shoe. I'm sure I was red-faced. I was always red-faced after taking a piss. Greatest effort of my day.

She didn't say anything, just nodded at the burly security guard who was holding a cardboard box labeled CHIQUITA BANANAS, which had all my accumulated stuff in it, including my EMPLOYEE OF THE QUAR-TER plaque. He showed me the way out.

I tossed the box in a nearby dumpster, jettisoned the contents of my stomach next to same, and stopped off in a Cicero tavern. I sat next to a man wearing a green Buy and Bye shirt, who had already hoisted a few according to the emptied pint and shot glasses next to him. "You look like shit."

"Thanks."

"Buy you one?"

"I can't say no, so I won't even bother to try."

We drank a couple of Old Styles and stared up at the TV hanging precariously from the ceiling above the bar. There were acoustic tiles just above the TV, stained a sort of burnt orange, like whoever pissed on them from the rafters above had blood in his urine. Somewhere in Arizona, men were playing baseball, while outside it was close to 30 below.

"Who's that?" I asked, nodding at the TV.

"Cubs."

"Cubs, huh?"

"Fuck the Cubs."

I agreed with him. Fuck the Cubs. He took that as an allegiance to the Southside, which I did nothing to discourage.

"So why are you day drinking?"

"Day drinking," I said, trying the idea on for size. It fit. "I got laid off. A guard escorted me from the building like I was a common criminal."

"Are you a criminal?"

"I am *not*. I am an American. I have rights."

"God damn right you do. Life, liberty, the pursuit of broads." We clinked glasses. The Cubs scored a run. "Fuck me in the heart."

"Rough day all around."

"You know it." He stood up. "I gotta get back to work. You need a job?"

"Fuck yeah, I need a job."

"You ever work at Buy and Bye?"

"I worked at the Buy and Bye on West Roosevelt for two years. Loved it."

"Clean record? Left under good circumstances?"

"Yes."

"Should be easy to rehire you then."

"Oh yeah?"

"Shit yeah. I'm the store manager at the Buy and Bye in Berwyn. Let's go."

I finished my beer and stood up, unsteadily. "Lead on, oh King eternal."

"Let's not get too excited. It's a warehouse job."

"Perfect. I'm done sitting at a desk like a common slob. I will lift things and carry them. I will put those things in their proper places. Like a man."

"That's the spirit, my friend. That's the spirit."

PRACTICE HUMILITY

Sometime after my second wife gave me the boot, I started wearing orthopedic shoes. You know the kind: Beige, with velcro instead of laces. It was a comfort thing. I may have been in my mid 30's by then. Or late 30's. I wore the same pair of khaki trousers most days, washing them every third day, until they fell off me, then I bought a new pair. I rotated between three camp shirts, no patterns, primary colors, and I bought black pocket t-shirts, sweat socks and white boxer shorts.

I'd settled into life. No wife, no pets—save the raccoon. But he was more like a roommate than a pet. We hung out together, watched whatever was on the tube. He danced a bit for the camera. We got views, and then we got paid. *Ch-Ching!* We ordered in pizza or Chinese. We irrigated our guts with cheap beer. It was cool.

Youth has desiccated out of me, turning me into a human jerky version of myself. I am mostly bald, so I buzz off what little hair grows on my head with an electric razor. A thicket of hair grows out of my earholes and nostrils, appearing every morning like some sort of mini-Chia Pet. I like it. Nothing to see here. Nothing at all.

I am nearly invisible to women. Not that I was all that visible to begin with. I'm bringing unsexy back.

I stood out on my lawn, looking out at about 100 or so people crowding my little street. I was ready for my first press conference or, as people call them in the business, my first presser.

The protesters had attracted counter-protesters. They carried signs with slogans like, IT'S JUST AN ANIMAL, STUPID.

There were five trucks from various news organizations parked up on curbs.

There was Congressional candidate Les Nunamaker, who stood in between the two sets of protesters, weighing which set of enthusiasts would get him the most votes. His youthful campaign workers handed out trifolds and bifolds and buttons and bumperstickers and sexy science fiction books written by Nunamaker himself and wore NUNAMAKER MAKING A DIFFERENCE t-shirts.

Sharma-LeenXXX, the sleepy-eyed star of Instagram, freshly chauffeured up from Miami, had knocked on my door earlier in the day. Her hair was currently an aquamarine blue. She breezed past me with her retinue, sucked in her cheeks and pouted while Bubby sat on the counter posing over her shoulder. She took selfies and then she and her people left without a word. Within the hour, Yahoo News called the bejeweled bra she had on in the photo "daring" and declared that she "owned Florida and all the people in it."

I would have looked up the post on Instagram myself, but I don't have an Instagram account. Not anymore. I'm not a fan of social media. I was on it once upon a time, until I wasn't. I can still, barely, remember an era when someone who left your life would stay left. Gone. Kaputski. Some gal who claims I knew her in high school friended me, and then kept posting her recollections about what a weirdo I was back then. What can you say to that? What's my reaction supposed to be amongst the tiny emoticons that are available below each post? Do I choose a heart? Do I choose a little "oh" face? The little steaming mad fellow? The thumbs-up? I had no reaction to it other than, why should I be reminded of who I was? I'm embarrassed. I wasn't much of a teenager. I wasn't much of a young adult. And present-tense me isn't any great shakes either. Let's say that I'm continually embarrassed about what a fender-bender of a human being I am. Not that I have the gumption to do anything about it. I went through the 20-step process to delete each of my accounts. I stay away from social media, save YouTube. The past should remain in the rearview mirror. It shouldn't keep arcing back around and cutting me off in traffic, flipping me the bird, squawking out, "Weirdo! Couch case! Nut bag!" I don't need reminding. I have a mirror at my disposal.

Chicken Wicket employees, dressed as black-spotted cows with pink udders, handed out samples of their new product, Extra Crunchy Fried Chicken Gloves with Honey Mustard or Hot Ranch dipping sauce. The first day the Chicken Wicket phony cows were outside, they had fake protest signs and had blended in with the actual protesters. The signs said, "PLEASE DON'T KILL ME, CHICKEN WICKET. MURDER THE CHICKENS INSTEAD." The next day, they were handing out the gloves. They gave me two gloves, one for myself and one for Bubby, so I shot a video of him putting it on—it looked ridiculously huge on his tiny hand—and Bubby devoured it. They slipped a check for $2,000 under my door the following day. In the memo line, it said, "MOO! DEATH TO CHICKENS!"

Whee! This was fun.

The Doug Liberty Bandit Girls, in the Doug Liberty Bandit Bug Volkswagen Beetle that had been cleverly painted and had prosthetics attached so that it looked like a giant raccoon, arrived each morning. The Doug Liberty Bandit Girls—dressed in gray hot pants with a bushy tail attached, noses painted black, whiskers glued to their faces, raccoon masks over their eyes and fake raccoon ears on their heads, wearing crop tops and high heels—hopped out of their Doug Liberty Bandit Bug (roomy enough to fit five girls!) and fired a pneumatic gun up over the crowd. Doug Liberty Presents Bandit the Dancing Raccoon t-shirts rained down on the good people of Sarasota's poorest neighborhood. Later, the Bandit Girls fired hot dogs into the air. They accidentally fired one through my front window and into Matka's display of Hummel figurines. Doug Liberty sent out a team to replace the window and vacuum up the shattered glass on the wall-to-wall carpeting, but there was no saving the little boy chimney sweep figurine, who'd been beheaded.

"I suppose I could glue the head back on," I told Bubby, after the workers had departed.

He shrugged and then farted. We both cracked up.

At some point, a stage appeared at the end of the street and a sound system was set up. Bubba Cartwright, a local crooner who'd had a top-ten hit in 1975 with "Smooth Carburetor," strummed the guitar and tried out his new material, in between playing "Smooth Carburetor" over and over and over. As the sun dipped down into the Gulf of Mexico, he gave way to his daughter, JuJu Cartwright, who was known as DJ Girly JuJu. She played dance mixes. I saw light sticks glowing as dry ice smoke drifted and foam sprayed out of unseen hoses at the revelers.

National Lawyers Guild legal observers, wearing suits, ties, and organizational baseball caps, squinted skeptically at the whole circus, taking extensive notes on yellow legal pads and shooting photos of the goings-on with cheap digital cameras when something looked amiss. They were there to protect us from my old classmate whatshisname. Let's call him Johnny Law from now on. Johnny Law was still hanging around, mostly observing the Doug Liberty Bandit Girls, keeping them in line, I guess, though he didn't stop them from killing off one of Matka's Hummel figurines with a pneumatically kinetic hot dog—the poor little headless chimney sweep. Elmer's Glue-All might fix him, but he'd never be truly whole again. Once you've lost your head, you never get it back, not really, not even when it's adhesed back on with America's favorite glue.

Let it go, Tris. Let it go.

"Can't sleep," I complained to Bubby, as we stared out the window at all those people, the front windows vibrating along with the bass beats. "The money's pretty good, so I shouldn't complain. How are you holding up? You need another beer?"

He nodded in the affirmative.

LaShonda Bagby showed up on the morning before my first press conference with a written statement that I was ordered to read to the assembled press outside at noon that day. She brought along a shirt and tie for me to wear. She insisted that I needed to tweez the hairs of out my ears, too. "You look like shit."

"Thanks. Noon?"

"For the noon news."

"Action news! Is the missus going to be there?"

"If you mean Mister Liberty's wife, Cassandra, then the answer is yes."

"Hot dog."

"Listen cueball," my raccoon's lawyer said, poking me in the chest with a sharp index fingernail, "don't you go leering at the boss's wife."

"Where's the harm?"

"You'll find that out once he has your legs broken."

"'I see,' said the blind man."

"Who cuts your hair?"

"I do. It's business in the front. Business in the rear. I'm all business."

"And no ad-libbing. How many beers have you had this morning?"

"I've lost count. How many have we had, Bubby?"

Bubby held up four tiny raccoon fingers.

"Oh for Christ's sake," LaShonda Bagby said, rolling her eyes.

"I'm fine. I'm not even a little tipsy."

"Can you read the statement? Is it in big enough type for you, drunky? Are you even capable of reading it?"

"I can read. I'm a reader." I shook out the paper and squinted at it. Maybe I needed to get a pair of drugstore cheaters at Eckerd's.

"Just out of curiosity, how can you drink so much beer and remain thin?"

"I'm full of nervous energy."

"I don't get that from you. You always seem so calm."

"That's from the beer."

I staggered out into my front lawn in my new shirt and tie at noon sharp, my ears and nostrils freshly tweezed, and held my sheet of paper out in front of me. There were words on it. A gaggle of reporters and camera persons crowded in front of me. It was dazzling. Even though it was broad daylight, little spotlights clicked on above their cameras, blinding me. I squinted at the sheet. I held it up to my face and read very quickly:

"On behalf of Doug Liberty Presents Bandit the Dancing Raccoon, I would like to express our appreciation for your outstanding coverage of this miracle of nature. The positive segments on the local and national news you gave this talented raccoon provided the community and the world with a great introduction to Doug Liberty Presents Bandit the Dancing Raccoon. Both Doug Liberty Presents Bandit the Dancing Raccoon and I appreciated the professionalism with which your news teams handled both the coverage of the protesters on our front lawn and the final studio presentation. Thanks for taking our side, guys! Viewer response on the Doug Liberty Presents Bandit the Dancing Raccoon channel on YouTube has dramatically increased since your newscasts. We hope to maintain this upward momentum with more quality entertainment on the Doug Liberty Presents Bandit the Dancing Raccoon channel on YouTube. As a longtime resident in this area, I am indeed grateful for your willingness to include us in your coverage. Please extend our thanks to everyone involved. I will take no questions. GO INSIDE. DO NOT TAKE QUESTIONS."

"Can we see your face?" Cassandra Liberty said.

"Pardon?" I lowered the sheet of paper and it blew out of my hand. I momentarily thought about chasing after it, but it blended in with all the discarded hot dog wrappers and campaign detritus.

"You had the sheet of paper in your face!" another reporter said angrily. "Mister Edgar, you're on three major cable networks, live, right now. We need a real statement for our viewers around the globe and in your neighborhood."

"And for your local news, thank you very much," Cassandra said.

"Who does a canned statement about a dancing raccoon?" another reporter said. "We're live! We've gone live and we've got nothing from you."

"Do you call him that all the time?" a fourth reporter asked.

"Call him what?" I asked.

"Doug Liberty Presents Bandit the Dancing Raccoon," the fourth reporter said.

"No. I call him 'Bubby.'"

"Bubby?" Cassandra went.

"Yeah. That's what he said his name was."

"Wait a minute. That raccoon can *talk*?" the second reporter said. "Are you nuts?"

"I'm not nuts. I'm drunk. There's a difference."

Cassandra leaned in enough that I got a good look into her considerable cleavage. "Shouldn't we be interviewing the raccoon? That is, *if* he can talk."

"He can talk. Not well, it's a little garbled, but he can talk."

That's when I felt the collar of my shirt being yanked backward, along with the rest of me.

"We'll take no further questions," LaShonda Bagby said, pulling me toward the house.

I stumbled over my own feet and fell onto my back, and the cameras leaned in. I saw nothing but sun, camera lenses and the soft black foam rubber tips on the business ends of the microphones.

"You have a talking raccoon inside that house?" the third reporter shouted. "That's a real story."

"He flies airplanes," I said, feeling crabgrass pushing its way through my new shirt.

"Get up!" LaShonda barked. "And shut up!"

"Who are you?" the second reporter asked.

"I'm LaShonda Bagby, attorney for Doug Liberty Presents Bandit the Dancing Raccoon."

"The raccoon needs a lawyer?" the fourth reporter asked.

"Everyone needs a lawyer!" LaShonda snapped. "This media availability is over."

The front door was wide open, and Bubby was standing in the middle of the passageway. Bubby got way up on his back legs, swayed from side-to-side and warbled out, "Hi! Muh num is.. Hi! Muh num is... Hi! Muh num is... Bubby Muck!" At least that's what it sounded like. And then he danced a bit, pretended to drop a mic and crossed his raccoon arms over his chest gangster style. I'd craned my neck to watch and LaShonda had lost her grip on my collar.

"Damn it!" LaShonda went.

"His name is Bubby Muck, and definitely not Slim Shady. You heard him," I said from my back in the warm, wet crabgrass, going blind from the midday Florida sun and news camera lights. "Didn't realize he had a last name until now. See? That's a fresh revelation. That's real news. That's a scoop! Aren't you glad you're live?"

LaShonda grabbed my wrists and pulled me across the lawn, across river gravel and over the top of a decorative bush, the cement front porch and through the front door, and into the foyer, and then slammed the front door shut in the faces of the assembled press corps.

"I think that went well," I said, climbing unsteadily to my feet. "Beer?" I wended my way to the kitchen and LaShonda followed me.

"No, I don't want a beer." LaShonda's phone rang. She looked at the phone as if it bit her, and then answered it. "Mister Liberty? Sir? ... No, sir, that wasn't planned... Yes, sir... No, sir..." I could hear him yelling, and yelling. She held the phone away from her head and winced. There was a loud click. "I'll take that beer now."

"That's the spirit." I pulled two Old Milwaukee Lights out of one of my 30 packs and handed her one. She stabbed her index fingernail right through the side of the can near the bottom, placed her lips on the spurting foam, pulled the tab and sucked the can dry in about ten seconds as the can collapsed. She tossed the crumpled-up empty at the sink, where it clinked around. "Phi Kappa Gamma," she said, by way of explanation. "You bled through the back of your new shirt."

"Oh."

"Give me a couple more beers and I'll put some iodine on the cuts."

"I'm fine."

"You're not fine. There's a lot of blood. I'm sorry."

"I don't feel it."

"How can you not feel it?"

"My body is of no interest to me other than as a thought experiment made flesh."

"What kind of overripe bullshit is that?"

"I dunno. Sounded good, though, didn't it? Did you know that you can order a crunch-wrap supreme with a couple of clicks on your phone and have it delivered? We live in miraculous times."

LaShonda sighed. "God give me strength."

Bubby climbed to his place on the counter. I gave him a swiggeroo out of my can.

"Bubby Muck!" I shouted at my raccoon pal. I put up my free hand near him and he high-fived me.

"Bubby Muck!" Bubby went. "Woot! Woot!"

"Beer, Tris. I was promised beer."

RESPECT CONSTRUCTIVE CRITICISM

When we were on the outs with each other, my soon-to-be-second-ex asked me, "Do you have to be awful? All the time?"

"I know of no other way to be, dear."

She didn't throw my clothes out of the window of our apartment. There was no melodrama.

Scratch that: It was never *our* apartment. It was *her* apartment. I was merely an extended guest there.

"You don't want to be responsible for anyone or anything. Not even yourself."

I didn't hesitate to reply. "Guilty."

She said, calmly, "You need to pack your shit and leave."

So I packed my shit and left.

A few things had to happen, were destined to happen, to prepare the road to my permanent singledom. It took about a year and half for me to completely screw up my marriage.

I'll elaborate.

First, I was fired from my job with benefits, and took, without LeeAnn's permission, a job without benefits at a Buy and Bye far from her Rogers Park apartment. I had to take the Red Line all the way down to the Loop, where I took the Blue Line all the way to the western end in Cicero, and I still had to walk a couple of miles to Berwyn after that.

I was fine with the commute and the job. LeeAnn was not.

LeeAnn had no appreciation of my alcoholism, having never experienced it. When I was with her, when she was around, I didn't feel the need to drink, so I did not. She never saw me drunk. She never saw me take a drink. When I told her that I'd been fired for coming in to work drunk, urinating on a fake plant, and passing out in a former bakery, she wasn't buying it at all.

"But you're a teetotaler." She was drying a dish after I'd washed it.

"Around you, sure."

"But I've never seen you take a drink, so you're not a drinker."

"That's an 'appeal to ignorance,' dear. *Argumentum ad ignorantiam.* A common logical fallacy."

"Are you calling me stupid?"

"No. Absolutely not. Ignorance isn't proof of anything except that one doesn't know something."

"Oh my God! You *are* calling me stupid!"

"Ignorance isn't the same as stupidity."

"Well, you're not all that bright yourself, so I don't know how you can call me stupid."

"That's an *ad hominem* attack. Another logical fallacy. But I wasn't calling you stupid before."

"You just did! Again!"

"Or maybe that was the *tu quoque* fallacy." I thought about it for a second. "No. It was *ad hominem*. I'm pretty sure of it."

She smashed the dish on the floor. "I'll *tu quoque*, you!" She cried and went into our bedroom, slamming the door shut behind her.

LeeAnn saved up some money from one of her photo shoots and ordered me via text message to meet her at her urologist's office. The address was in the message.

I called her up. I was on a break and hanging with some of my co-workers at a juice bar in the same strip mall as the Buy and Bye. I was having a Mango Supreme Surprise, which was mostly sugar in a suspension of fruit pulp, some of which was mango. "I was unaware that you had a urologist, dear." I slurped a bit of the Mango Supreme Surprise through the green straw and felt high ten seconds later. When I'm not drinking, I consume approximately a shit-ton of sugar.

"We used to have health insurance. I had access to all sorts of doctors. Now I want you to use this one."

"Oh? What for?" Slurp, slurp.

"We're going to make sure that I don't get knocked up. Snip, snip."

"Oh?" I involuntarily pulled my knees together and gritted my teeth. Mango-flavored sugar goo bubbled up my esophagus and back into my mouth. It didn't taste as good the second time around.

"If you don't show up at the appointed time, there will be dire consequences."

"Yes, dear."

When I got to the doctor's office, about 15 minutes late, I was whisked through a couple of sets of doors. A woman wearing a pink surgical get-up was waiting for me. So was LeeAnn.

"Your wife says that you agreed to her being in the room with us. She's sterile."

"If she's sterile, then why am I getting the old snip-a-rooski?"

"See? I told you," LeeAnn said to the doctor, like the two of them were best friends. Maybe they were. I didn't know any of LeeAnn's friends. "Shitty jokes. Nothing but shitty jokes. He thinks he's being cute. He thinks he's funny. Who'd want to have a kid with someone like that?"

The urologist, whose name I didn't catch, told me to disrobe. I did so and put on a proffered surgical gown.

"I see you already shaved," the urologist noted.

"Last night. It was for sexual adventure, the wife told me." She'd also given me a pill that was supposed to heighten the sexual experience, but it caused me to pass out and forget almost everything. I awoke with a thudding hangover.

"That's silly." LeeAnn smiled crookedly in a way that suggested I should never trust her again. "You signed all the consent forms. We discussed this last night."

"Oh." I suppose I could have slipped my pants back on and made a break for it. I didn't. "Let's get on with this then." I'd never been operated on before. The last time I was under treatment, I was six. I was curious. Adventure!

"Good boy." She ran her hand across my thinning hair.

Another pink-clad surgical woman came in and put an I/V into my arm. Another pink-clad surgical woman injected something into the I/V. I felt calm. I was exposed from the waist down on a cold metal table. I felt pinpricks. Strangely, I felt the cut into my sack and the rooting around. It didn't bother me like I thought it should. Thank you, pharmaceutical companies of America! LeeAnn stood alongside the doctor, staring at my junk while the doctor caused me to be non-reproductive.

Afterward, LeeAnn helped me put my clothes back on and helped me walk down to the EL. I was dizzy. Everything seemed unreal. I was in a videogame of my life. We rode a few stops, and then she walked me back to the apartment we shared, took all of my clothes off, and put me to bed. I fell into a deep sleep.

The following morning, she told me that she'd called in sick for me for the rest of the week. "What do you want to eat, sweetie?"

"I'm not hungry."

"Don't pout. It was for your own good. You'd be a terrible father. You know it. I know it. Everyone who has ever met you knows it."

"I'd like some jello."

"I'll see if we have some." She handed me a bag of frozen peas. "So your pee-pee doesn't get too swollen."

I heard her leave. She came back a half-hour later. She shouted from the other room, "I had to go buy some jello. I hope you like cherry."

"Cherry is good."

She came in the room with a water bottle and a pill. I recognized the pill. It was the same one that caused me to sign the consent forms. "This will help."

I took the pill and drank the water.

At some point, I awoke. I felt weirdly depleted and oily. I had a lanolin scent to me, like a baby wipe. My tongue was coated with a chemist's idea of what a cherry should taste like. And I was horny. LeeAnn, I realized, was giving me a handjob under the sheet. "Good boy. Come for mama. Come for me." I came hard. I felt a piece of cold plastic near my dick. Then I heard a top being screwed on. LeeAnn kissed me on the forehead and shook a clear plastic jar of my ejaculate at me. "Now we can have great sex again, as long as you don't have any wigglers in your spoo. Unless you think I'm too stupid to have sex with a genius like you."

"I never called you stupid," I said, panting. "I never called myself a genius."

"Let's not argue, or I'll pull your stitches out for you early."

"Yes, dear."

LeeAnn decided that the solution to our marital problems was to run away from them to the state where I got my first divorce. Viva Las Vegas! LeeAnn got an assignment to shoot the National Broadcasters convention. She would be one of five photographers to wander around the convention taking photos of conventioneers and people manning the booths. She received two passes with colorful lanyards. Hers announced her as PHOTOGRAPHER. Mine announced me as GUEST.

We checked in at the hotel. It was the oldest one on the strip. There was a casino next to the check-in desk. I peered around. The place was filled with celebrity impersonators, but I had trouble figuring out which celebrities they were supposed to be.

"Is that guy a bankrobber?" I asked, pointing at one. "A cop?"

"No," LeeAnn said, rolling her eyes. "He's supposed to be one of the Blues Brothers."

"Which one?" He wasn't fat enough to be Jake, and wasn't tall enough to be Elwood.

"Who cares? Why do you care?" LeeAnn snapped.

"I don't know. Are you going to be angry at me the whole time?"

"Only when you're acting like a child. You don't have to be a child all the time. And if you tell me about logical fallacies or what Kant would say, I'm going to smack you right in front of Madonna there."

"That's Cindy Lauper."

"That's Madonna."

"Let's ask her."

"Let's not. Let's check in and go up to our room."

We followed a guy hauling our luggage for us who looked like Steve Buscemi in *Barton Fink*. We went to the elevator, and then to our room, which overlooked nothing. That's not quite right. It overlooked the white wall of another building ten feet next door. He dumped our bags in the middle of the room and then held out his hand to me.

LeeAnn hip-checked me out of the way and handed him several ones.

"Steve Buscemi. Right?" I nodded at him so he'd agree.

He didn't. "Why do people keep saying that to me?"

"My name is Chet! Chet!" I went.

"You're an embarrassment," my wife said to me. To Chet: "Please ignore him."

"Avoid all woodchippers, Chet."

LeeAnn handed the Steve Buscemi lookalike another couple of bills. "Thank you. Have a nice day." He hurriedly exited the room.

I plopped down on the bed as the door closed. It was as comfortable as a slab of concrete. "Glad your employer didn't overspend on the room." A weird scent lingered around the bed. I got up and tore off the sheets. The mattress featured an oval brown stain in the shape of a body. Or maybe a deer had been butchered.

"You can complain, if you want." LeeAnn stood next to me, smiling wickedly.

"I can take it if you can take it."

"I can take it."

I pulled off her shirt and popped open her bra. I pushed her onto the bed, right in the middle of the stain. I tore off her skirt and panties, and then pulled one sneaker off her, then the other, tossing them across the room. She giggled and kicked at me. I stripped and we had aggressive sex on top of the itchy mattress, each taking a turn being on top. Afterward, we lay facing one another, poking each other as we conjectured who may have died in our room, on our bed.

"One in the heart and two in the hat."

"Blam, blam!" she went, making pistols out of her hands.

"Nicky Santoro."

"Tommy DeVito."

"Leo Getz."

"Vinnie Gambini."

"David Ferrie."

"Jimmy Alto."

"Louie Kritski."

Poke, poke, poke. We remade the bed, turned on the TV, lay nude together and watched a tutorial on how to play blackjack. "Our fortune is made," I said.

"You're not playing blackjack."

"Our fortune is unmade."

"I'll unmake you." She quickly straddled me. "Round two?"

"It's on like Donkey Kong."

The next morning, we ate breakfast at the MGM Grand, $20 for all-you-can-eat for the both of us, and then took a bus to the convention hall. LeeAnn released me on my own recognizance. We each had flip phones. "I'll call you when it's time to go."

I walked the floors, stopping to rubberneck at booths where small producers were pitching TV shows for syndication. Mostly, it was talk shows featuring standup comedians, judges and pop psychologists.

A dominatrix stood in the middle of my path as I wended my way around. "Excuse me," I said.

She cracked a whip on the floor. "Crawl worm!"

"Not my thing."

"I know my prey. You're my prey."

"It's a common mistake. I'm not weak. I'm not anything." I looked over at her booth. The name of her show was, *Carol Knows Discipline!* I sauntered over and read her sign, and then picked up a flyer. "WEEKNIGHTS AFTER DARK, CAROL WILL TAKE ON ALL WEAK MEN AND MAKE THEM OBEY."

"So what do you think?" Carol asked.

"I think you have a winner." I pocketed the flyer. "We'll be in touch."

She kissed me on the cheek, leaving behind a ruby red blotch. "Thank you, thank you, thank you!"

A few booths down, I found a children's show set in an underground bunker filled with barrels of freeze-dried food and munitions. *The Mr. Clark Show* featured a man in a bumble bee costume who was in the middle of his monologue as I walked up and sat down. "Fight the globalist agenda with me, children," he said, sitting down on a box of ammunition. "Don't worry about me, kids. There are armed snipers up on the top floor to protect your old pal Mister Clark." He wiped a single tear from his cheek. His face was the only thing not covered in bee costume. He wore white gloves and oversized shoes, and yellow and black hosiery on his arms and legs. "Mister Clark only wants to give you the unfiltered truth of his soul. That truth is: Your parents can't save you, children. Only these Maximum Power candy cigarettes can." He handed out boxes of cigarettes from a single carton to the audience members, who represented various independent television stations from around the country. I looked at the cigarette box when he handed it to me. It was labeled, VITAMIN PACKED SUPER MENTHOL and had a picture of a winking bee on it. "Remember to practice every day with your Power Pop Laser Enhanced Toy Guns with real pneumatic action." He handed a single replica of an Uzi to one audience member, who turned it over in his hands for a moment and passed it on. "Study *The Big Coloring Book of Conspiracy*, and learn how to identify crisis actors." He handed the book to another audience member, and it made its way around the room. "Practice the no-fluoride lifestyle now, kids, by using my no-fluoride toothpaste, Wonder Gel. Look under your seats." I reached under my seat and found a plastic bag with about a half-dozen give-aways in it, including the useless toothpaste. "Your teachers lie to you constantly. They're paid by the state. Question everything they say." I placed the little bag along with the candy cigarettes under my chair and quietly walked away.

I found LeeAnn before she had the opportunity to call me. She seemed surprised that I would seek her out. "I thought you'd be in your element with all these weirdos."

"I'm good."

"What's on your cheek?"

"Residue from a future TV star. She cracked a whip at me."

"Carol."

"Yeah. Carol."

We left and walked down the strip together. "You'll have to give me a shoulder rub when we get back."

I took her camera bag and hung it around my shoulder for a while. It weighed a ton. "How do you carry this around all the time?"

"You get used to it."

"I wouldn't."

A sly little man walked up to us with a card. He snapped it over and over and held it out to me. I took it. It was an advertisement for a prostitution firm that would deliver a "fresh girl" to your room. All you needed to do was call the number on the card.

I handed it to LeeAnn. "Threesome?"

She flipped it onto the sidewalk, where there were piles of them. "Fuck you."

A month later, Pop called me up in Chicago and told me that I needed to come home to Florida.

"What's going on?"

"Your grandmother. She's ill."

"Fatally?"

"How should I know? Get down here."

I told LeeAnn. I told Buy and Bye. LeeAnn came home with groceries and two tickets to Florida.

"You're coming along?"

"I've never met your family."

"I've never met yours."

"That's different."

"How?"

"I don't like mine." She smirked at me.

"You won't feel any different about my grandparents. They're closed off. They don't like outsiders."

"I'm going with you, poopsy. End of discussion."

We were separated on the flight.

Shortly before take-off, I called her up from my flip phone and said in a cutesy voice, "I wuv you. Do you wuv me?"

"Are you trying to sound like...? Oh my God. You're a hateful person! You're a dumpster fire. You know that? A dumpster fire." She slapped the phone shut, got up from her seat, turned around and glared angrily at me.

I grinned and waved at her. I felt my marriage failing. I wanted to give it a little push in that direction. Embrace failure as a way of life.

We took a cab from Sarasota-Bradenton International Airport to my grandparents' place a few miles away. "There's the Bahi Hut," I said, pointing out the Tiki-themed dive bar. "We'll go there later and drink a Mai Tai together and imagine that we're on a tropical island instead of in Florida."

"I'm not talking to you," she said.

"Dude, your old lady is bumming me out," the cab driver said. He was a mass of unwashed and uncombed hair, wearing a Florida State hoodie with the sleeves cut off, jams and flip-flops. His teeth were various shades of brown. At the airport, he'd stood and watched as we loaded our own luggage into the trunk of his gypsy cab, a

Ford Gran Torino painted metallic blue with the phone number spray-stenciled on the driver's side door. He'd been tanning non-stop since childhood, by the look of him.

"She's doing the same for me."

"Don't you recognize me, dude?"

"Should I?"

"We went to high school together."

"Okay."

"We were in kiltie band together. Remember? You played the clarinet. I played the baritone."

"You know why I didn't recognize you? You've changed. It used to be all about the music. Now you're just a hack."

"I hate you," LeeAnn said. "And I hate the cab driver. Florida smells like mold. Who the fuck would voluntarily live down here?"

"Now your old lady is trashing the Sunshine State. She's bumming me the fuck out, dude."

I reached over his shoulder and handed him a twenty, the equivalent of two hours' work at Buy and Bye. "Step on it. She needs to get to my house so she can bum out my grandparents."

"Awesome sauce."

Matka sat at the dining room table in her housecoat. She looked like hell. She'd lost a third of her body weight and what little hair she had left had gone completely white. "Chemo and radiation. *Neni mi dobre.*"

We sat down in chairs on either side of her. She had an open container of yogurt in front of her, undisturbed. "He's no help."

"Pop?"

"Who else?"

"This is my wife LeeAnn. You've spoken to her on the phone once or twice."

"I asked for you to come home, not her."

"We're married," LeeAnn said by way of explanation.

"Her photos don't do her justice. My God, she's homely," Matka said to me. "You could have married a fat one with a pretty face. At least there's a chance the fat one could lose weight."

"I'm going to pretend you didn't say that because you're sick," LeeAnn said.

"Go right ahead and do whatever you want," Matka said.

I tried to change the subject by telling her about our trip to Las Vegas. I ended the story with the anecdote about the guy handing out the prostitution flyers.

"But you didn't need a prostitute." Matka turned and looked directly at LeeAnn. "You already had one."

My mistake was—and it was a pretty big one—laughing at the horrible joke, and then trying to tamp the laughter back down in my throat, which made me choke a bit.

Matka saw me laughing and laughed herself, loud and unrestrained.

LeeAnn's face turned red and she stood up and stomped out of the room.

"Shit," I went.

"You're in big trouble."

"So are you."

"Cancer is my only trouble. I don't care about your homely wife. You could have done better, but that old man in the other room didn't give a shit about you. He could have told you to better yourself, instead he told you to become a drain on the system. You could have been a teacher. You could have been so much more than a bum."

"True enough. I am a bum. But I don't blame anyone but myself."

"Chemo burned every bit of restraint I have. So I'm sorry I said... No—*wait*. I'm not sorry. Not a bit sorry."

"Matka, I'm sorry I wasted my life."

"You should be."

"Can you apologize to her? For me?"

"No. I'm done apologizing. I'm sick. I'm dying. I'll go to the afterlife with a clear conscience. I hope they speak Czech there."

"Why?"

"Because I'm Czech."

"Oh. I always thought you were Cuban. I guess I could get in trouble for putting 'hispanic' on all those application forms over the years."

"Ugh. You're as hispanic as Jeb Bush, you dummy."

Our marriage didn't survive the trip. Not really. But Matka did. She lingered on for years and years, going in and out of remission.

After LeeAnn gave me the boot, I couch-surfed for months. I said to one co-worker after another at Buy and Bye, "Mind if I crash on your couch for a week or two? Landlord kicked me out for forgetting to pay my rent."

I was a gypsy. I *am* a gypsy.

Did I forget to mention that I am an actual gypsy? Father's side.

About six months after LeeAnn asked me to leave, a process server found me loitering outside of a hipster tavern in Logan Square. I'd followed a woman who looked just like Delores, my first wife, there. But she was too young to be Delores. I sat down at a small, circular table in the crowded room and waited for someone to wait on me. The Delores lookalike came out of the backroom wearing a stained bar apron. "That's him!" she said, pointing at me.

The room quickly turned. Everyone was staring in my direction. "What?" I went.

"He's been following me!"

"Me? Following?" But I'm not a good enough liar when it really counts. They all could tell. All those hipster eyes, staring.

I got up and walked outside, where the process server was leaning against a light pole covered over in band flyers for concerts at the Empty Bottle. "Tristram Edgar?"

"Guilty."

"You're a hard one to track down." He handed me a manila envelope. "If you don't mind my saying, you look like shit."

"Thanks."

"Take care of yourself, man. No one else will." He turned on his heel and sprinted away.

"I need a drink." I always needed a drink then. I continue to need a drink today. I am drinking right now. Cheers! I opened the envelope and found divorce papers inside, along with a court date, two days in the future.

I showed up at the Cook County courthouse at the appointed time outside of the correct courtroom. I was not drunk, not even a bit tipsy. LeeAnn was there, accompanied by an attorney whose stunning body graced a billboard off the Dan Ryan expressway. On the billboard, she was draped across a bearskin rug wearing a satin teddy.

She stared out at passing cars with come-hither eyes, her manicured hand in her flowing blonde hair, licking her full painted lips. The legend on the billboard read: "DIVORCE is HARD!!! Mary Jo Kowalski... on the job FOR YOU!"

In court, Mary Jo Kowalski had that blonde hair pinned up and was sheathed in a sexless, gray business pantsuit.

"You hired the billboard lawyer?" I asked LeeAnn.

"You made fun of her so much that I almost had to. Did you read the divorce papers?"

"I skimmed them."

"I'm not asking for anything from you, because you don't have anything. Just sign the papers in front of the judge and we can get on with our lives."

"Okay."

"When did you buy the old man shoes?"

"I dunno. They're comfortable."

"You couldn't put on a tie?"

"I don't own one."

"I hope your grandmother is well."

"She hates you."

"Luckily, I'm a bigger person than she is."

"Physically, sure."

"And in every other way you can imagine. She's a horrible, terrible person."

"Who you hope is well."

"Because I'm a better person than she is. I'm sure she wishes me dead."

Mary Jo Kowalski, attorney at law, said, "Stop talking. Both of you."

"Yes, ma'am," I said, picturing her up on that sign.

"You're picturing her on the sign," LeeAnn said.

"Yep."

"Quiet!" Mary Jo waved us into the courtroom behind her. I was both frightened by the courtroom and sexually excited by my wife's attorney.

We were summoned before the judge, an older man who leered at Mary Jo. "Good to see you, counselor."

Mary Jo smirked. "Your honor."

He returned the smirk. "So I see that everything is in order? Do you two agree?"

"Yes, your honor," I said.

"Yes, your honor," LeeAnn said.

"I'm going to read this divorce settlement line by line. I want you both to agree to each stipulation and then initial next to it. At the end, you'll both sign."

Mary Jo handed each of us a Bic Clic.

"Yes, your honor." LeeAnn choked up a bit.

"Yes, your honor." I did not choke up.

As the judge read each line, I felt a massive weight lifting off my chest, a weight that, until that moment, I didn't realize was crushing me to death. I felt lighter and lighter.

LeeAnn wept a bit as each line was read. Her voice broke more with each "Yes, your honor."

Then the judge said, "That's it. That'll be forty-nine dollars and eighteen cents. Sign the divorce papers and pay the clerk."

Mary Jo handed LeeAnn an envelope with paper and metal money in it. LeeAnn handed it to the clerk. We took turns signing the papers.

"You're now officially divorced." The gavel came down. Pow!

The three of us left the courtroom. I felt like the center of my chest was filled with helium, like someone might have to grab my ankles before I floated away.

LeeAnn broke down crying, her head bowed with grief. I reached over to pat her on the back, and she shrugged me off. "Get away from me, you asshole!"

"Oh, that's right. I don't have to do that anymore," I said aloud. "I feel light as a cloud."

"Now you can go ruin someone else's life!" she shouted at me.

"Nope. The best part of this is that I never have to do it again. Finished. My dating days are kaput." I danced a little jig, right there in the courthouse hallway. "Done-ditty-done-done-done."

"Stay away from my client," Mary Jo said, angrily. "And stay away from women. You're toxic."

"No problem."

Mary Jo placed her arm around the weeping LeeAnn and led her away.

LeeAnn wrote me an email a few months after our divorce, detailing all the things I'd done wrong, calling me juvenile, calling me shallow. She said that she thought I was "semi-autistic" and being married to me was like "one, long, retarded pajama party." Her email was strident and accusatory, everything I discovered that I didn't like about her once I was free of her. I pointed out the tenor of her email to her in a reply, and she replied that, upon reading her previous email, that she was not strident and accusatory at all. Just the opposite.

"You hate me," she accused in the return email. "You left me because I'm homely."

She was wrong there. I may have called her homely at some point, but on the list of reasons why I wasn't with her anymore, that didn't even make the top ten. She had a cloud of self-hatred following her around like a personal disease that infected people around her. I didn't even know how much I hated myself until I lived with her for a couple of years.

But I didn't hate her. She was wrong there. I wrote an email in reply to hers that started out: "I don't hate you. I *nothing* you." I deleted that part right away, despite its accuracy. It was too mean. So I wrote, "There's the me that I am, and the me that you want me to be. I'm done being that other man." The email was larded up with philosophical nonsense, just like me. But interacting with her in any way was exhausting, so I deleted the email and sent no reply. We'd wasted each other's time enough in life. There was nothing left there. Nothing to see. Move along.

She writes me on occasion about things that I think she imagines that I imagine I am expert in—essay writing, logic conundrums, who to contact at Buy and Bye for returning a blender, and so on. The emails bring back the old feelings. I remember those sharp pangs of desire. I remember her doggedness. I remember the warmth and softness of her skin. I remember her being in the room while a surgeon cut into my ball sack. I remember her telling me that she loved me, which, in retrospect, I don't believe at all.

Good, bad... these memories are all the same.

I don't want to feel the old feelings.

I don't want to feel a thing.

I keep responding. They're short responses. But still.

I have to stop responding, otherwise the emails will never end.

"I'm telling you, Bubby, you haven't lived until you've eaten a Cheez Whiz on Eggo sandwich."

He turned his nose up a bit.

"C'mon. You're a raccoon. This is in your wheelhouse."

The two frozen waffles popped up out of the toaster and I spread a godly sized dollop of Cheez Whiz on one, sprinkled some bacon bits on, and plopped the other waffle on top. I set it on the counter near him. Bubby sniffed skeptically at it, and then quickly wolfed it down.

"Good, right?"

"Meh," the raccoon went with a shrug.

"We'll get another one of those chicken gloves later. I think they're still giving them away out front."

I clicked on the tube and caught the local news. It was day four of raccoon fest out there, and it had turned ugly for Congressional candidate Les Nunamaker, who was caught on camera performing inappropriate hugging of Sharma-LeenXXX, the sleepy-eyed star of Instagram. He'd sidled up alongside her during a set by the Pop Stoppers on the mainstage. There were now three stages on our street. During their hit "Lump of Flesh," Les' campaign photographer took a photo of him placing his arm around Sharma-LeenXXX, and then uploaded it to Instagram, where it caused an internet firestorm. Analysts both inside and outside the Channel 42 Southwest Florida's Independent Television Station studio made much of how close his hand was to one of her breasts. Experts in micro-expressions broke down Sharma-LeenXXX's reaction. To the layperson, her face didn't appear to change from photo to photo (sleepy eyes, puckered mouth, chin down), but to those in the know, she was devastated. Her Instagram, according to the experts who'd analyzed it, also gave away that she was "totally destroyed," judging by the lack of its usual exuberance. Typical post-hug post: "Hangin' in tha Sota, whut? (three sushi emojis followed by three poop emojis)."

Nunamaker's campaign released a denial, followed by a formal apology, followed by a statement by his wife supporting him, followed by the news that he'd checked himself into a facility to be treated for sexual addiction.

Bubby snorted, unimpressed by the brouhaha. He pointed at the Xbox with a flight simulator installed we'd received from one of his fans. I hadn't taken it out of the box yet. "Fly," he mewled. "Fly."

I opened the box and was immediately confused by all the wires, the controllers, and a bar that I think was some sort of camera. "I don't know about installing this thing," I said. "We need better internet, the hard-wired kind. Maybe Mister Liberty will get us some good internet. I can't keep stealing it from the neighbors."

"Bah," Bubby went. He hopped off the couch and made his way to the box. "Fly."

I pulled everything out and Bubby yanked on the wires and arranged them neatly on the floor.

"Maybe someone outside has a handle on all this. I think I saw a GoCast cable truck out there."

"Bubby Muck. Bubby Muck fly."

"Yeah, yeah. Let me check on the beer situation." I opened the fridge and leaned in. Our two 30 packs were considerably depleted. "And there was sadness across the land. May have to make a beer run later. I gotta dodge that one clerk at the Eckerd's though. I haven't signed up for their special discount club yet. He might get upset with me."

"Pants," Bubby bleated.

I looked down. Sure enough, I'd neglected to put on pants. I was wearing my boxers and a pair of mismatched socks. "Thanks, man."

I went back to my bedroom and found Bubby's lawyer climbing in through my window. "Hey," I went.

"Damn, boy. Put on some pants," LaShonda Bagby said as she knocked over the lamp on my dresser.

I caught the lamp and offered her a hand, which she waved off. "I came back here to put on some pants. Didn't expect to find a lawyer letting herself in."

She put the screen back on the window and straightened herself out while I hopped into my khakis and velcro-ed my shoes in place. "You ever read your email? You should look in your inbox every once in a while."

"I don't require Canadian Viagra, so I don't look very often."

"Maybe if you got some Canadian Viagra, you'd have a girlfriend."

"My dating days are over. My days of giving a shit are over."

"Clearly," she said, gesturing up and down at me. "What the fuck kind of thirty-eight-year-old man wears this? You're dressed for the nursing home."

"I'm thirty-eight? Could have sworn I made it to forty by this time." I shrugged. "Onward and upward. I take it you're here to see your client. Bubby says that he wants cable and internet. Who are you to deny him these basic necessities of life?"

"Aren't you demanding this morning?" I'd coaxed a rare smile out of LaShonda. "I'll talk to Mister Liberty."

"I'm merely Bubby Muck's valet."

"Stop calling him that. You know his name."

"So does the entire world."

"If you'd read your email, you'd know that a limo is heading this way. We're going to the game today."

"Nice. I haven't been to a Bucs game in a while. Who's the quarterback these days? Is it that guy from FSU? Or is it the old backup from the Bills?"

"We're not going to the Buccaneers game."

"What other game is there?"

"There's the Tampa Bay Trash Pandas. They play in the Saint Pete Thunderdome."

"The Tampa Bay what?"

"They're part of the Women's American Football League. Mister Liberty is the owner. He's arranged for Doug Liberty Presents Bandit the Dancing Raccoon to be out on the field for the ceremonial coin toss against our archrivals, the Atlanta Kudzus. Then we'll retire to the owner's suite for the game."

"Waffle," I went.

"Waffle?"

"Women's American Football League. Waffle."

"No wonder your wives dumped you."

"I'm a two-time loser."

The limo arrived at the periphery of the masses of people who'd congregated out front. I carried Bubby in my arms, wading through all these people, some of whom reached out to touch him like he was risen Jesus. He snarled and snapped at the outstretched hands, unless they were attached to good-looking women.

I took note of the many factions. First, and foremost, there were the protesters against my exploitation of Bubby. They booed as I walked through them on my front driveway. Then there were the counterprotesters, who were all for my exploitation of Bubby. They cheered and raised up hands while I walked past. Alongside them were the people protesting that anyone was protesting about a mere raccoon. Then there were the Chicken Wicket fake cow protesters, waving their fried chicken-gloved hands, who had real vegan protesters protesting Chicken Wicket. "Meat is murder!" Semi-nude protesters body-painted as sexualized raccoons held up a banner, "POST-FURRIES FOR RACCOON-TRANSHUMANIST LOVE." There were protesters against Les Nunamaker, who wore pink pussy hats, and protesters for him, who claimed to be for men's rights—STOP OPPRESSING TESTOSTERONE was their banner. Another group congregated under a sign that read GALATIANS 4:8. They knelt, joined hands and prayed for Bubby, possibly. Or maybe they were praying against Bubby.

Every last person out there, save those praying, had a phone in their hand, holding it up, making videos of Bubby. Some had their backs turned to us, so they could have their faces in the foreground of the video with Bubby in the background. Others straight-up shot Bubby. They held the phones above their heads, clusters of outstretched hands holding phones, and all the people staring into the screens of the phones instead of directly at us, staring at videos of Bubby, and the unsmiling bald guy dressed like a geriatric carrying the raccoon.

At the edge, near the limo, was Johnny Law, my old high school classmate, who stood grinning and clad in riot gear like a latter-day Roman centurion. He was the only cop around.

"Get you anything? Cup of coffee?" I asked him.

He set down his riot shield, raised the face guard of his helmet with his freed hand and then slapped me on the arm. "You look like shit."

"Thanks."

"Good to see you again. Good to have you home where you belong."

"Good to be back, I guess. I don't understand why people are so fascinated."

"All this will all quiet down, eventually," he said matter-of-factly. "You'll see. Something new will happen. A new shiny object. Then you'll have peace and quiet. You can go get a job."

"Heaven forfend."

"That's the spirit. People need simple answers for complicated questions, and complicated answers for simple questions. They think your talking raccoon may provide simple answers. Or maybe that he provides a complexity to our under-complex existence."

"We even have people calling upon our Lord for some reason."

"'Formerly, when you did not know God, you were slaves to those who by nature are not gods.'"

"What?"

"Galatians Four-Eight. I looked it up on my Bible app."

"Ah."

He flipped down the face guard and picked up his shield. "Get in your limo. Your luxury box awaits."

"Yes, officer."

The limo was a stretch Fiat 500, which was called a Fiat 1000. A magnetic sticker clinging to the passenger-side door announced one of the occupants in Helvetica Bold: Doug Liberty Presents Bandit the Dancing Raccoon. Bubby and I were the last in.

I found myself sitting next to one of the Bandit Girls, facing the rear window. She was not wearing the makeup or the headgear, but was wearing kneepads, shoulder pads and cleats, in addition to a crop top with 99 printed on the front. She still had on the hot pants with the tail attached, which I accidentally sat on as I slid in next to her. Four people barely fit inside the back of the stretch Fiat. We shut the doors. The woman I was sitting next to knocked on the window next to her head and said, "Let's light this candle."

I was facing LaShonda, who was sitting next to her client. I was trying not to be distracted by my seatmate's legs.

"May I pet him?" the Bandit Girl asked.

"Not up to me," I said. "Bubby's his own raccoon. You could ask his lawyer." I nodded at LaShonda, who rolled her eyes.

In answer, Bubby crawled onto the Bandit Girl's lap and made happy gurgling noises as she ran her fingers through his pelt. "He smells like my grandpa."

"He's fond of Vitalis."

Bubby turned in her lap and placed his head upon her considerable breasts. And then he fucking winked at me.

LaShonda reached behind her seat and fished out a tiny t-shirt for Bubby and a larger one for me. PROPERTY OF TAMPA BAY TRASH PANDAS. The team colors were a swirl of purple, orange, red and blue, like someone had left random crayons on top of a water heater and they'd all melted together. The t-shirts were dizzying to look at.

The Bandit Girl helped Bubby putting his on. I held mine in my lap. LaShonda dug around in the back and found a tiny Trash Pandas bucket hat for Bubby, and he put it on. "Gooo-ooo-ooo tee-ee-m," he went. He got a little excited and danced a bit in the Bandit Girl's lap, accidentally tearing her fishnet stockings.

"Sorry about that," I said, pointing.

"It's okay," she said. "They get pretty torn up during the games."

"You're a player?" I asked.

"I'm the quarterback. I also play linebacker. We all play both ways."

"Sorry I didn't recognize you."

"That's okay. I didn't recognize you at first either. You look different from TV. Younger."

"I thought you were one of the Bandit Girls."

"I am. I'm not making a lot of money with the football team. I also sell cars at Mister Liberty's lot in Nokomis."

Having exchanged niceties, the two of us simultaneously turned and stared out of opposite windows. LaShonda stared into her phone.

We went up US 301 to US 19, and then took the Sunshine Skyway bridge over to St. Petersburg. We ended up in where the old historic district used to be. The quaint old Floridian homes had been flattened to make way for the Doug Liberty Presents the St. Petersburg Thunderdome. It looked like a massive marshmallow on the outside. Sickly palm trees jutted up around the entrance, the fronds turned an appalling shade of yellow. The limo took us to the entrance. We came to a halt, and the quarterback bolted from the vehicle. She came back a few seconds later and leaned in. "I'll throw a touchdown pass for you today," she told Bubby, and scratched him behind the ear.

"Gooo-ooo-ooo tee-ee-m," he went.

An intern, also dressed up as a sexualized human-raccoon hybrid, took us through the bowels of the stadium. Inside, it looked less like a marshmallow and more like a basement in Chicago. It also had a basement funk to it. The gray-painted cinderblock walls dripped with moisture. The floor was covered over in a thick, black, non-skid coating. The hallways were filled with unnatural light. I carried Bubby in my arms. He was getting heavy.

We came upon the rest of the team in a tunnel. They jogged in place, warming up, their raccoon tails twitching from side to side. A stadium announcer's voice boomed out: HERE THEY ARE! DOUG LIBERTY PRESENTS YOUR TAMPA BAY TRASH BANDITS. There were multiple explosions. An air raid siren went off. The women sprinted ahead of us. The intern looked at her tablet, and then pointed at the field. "Go," she said. The stadium announcer's voice boomed out: WITH SPECIAL GUEST DOUG LIBERTY PRESENTS BANDIT THE DANCING RACCOON.

I ran the best I could out toward the middle of the field. I soon got winded, and Bubby leapt out of my arms. He trotted three feet, threw up his hands and did a Nixonian salute to the crowd, and then trotted another three feet and danced, and so on. The entire stadium was eating it up. I continued to follow him out, until the intern caught up with me and escorted me to the sideline.

"You're not needed," she said, consulting her tablet. "Doug Liberty Presents Bandit the Dancing Raccoon has great instincts. Mister Liberty wants this to play out. I'll take you to the owner's box. Follow me."

I peered around. No LaShonda. The stadium, which seated 30,000 people, was full of cheering fans by the look of it, most of them wearing Trash Panda products.

From the rafters, a massive American flag unfurled, nearly dipping all the way down to the field.

The stadium announcer's voice boomed out: BETSY JO HURLBURT, A RESIDENT OF DUNEDIN, WILL NOW SING THE NATIONAL ANTHEM. The lights dimmed and a grade school aged girl dressed up like a sexualized raccoon stepped onto a pedestal that was rolled out by similarly dressed interns. AS ALWAYS, NO KNEELING IS ALLOWED IN THE DOUG LIBERTY PRESENTS THE SAINT PETERSBURG THUNDER-DOME DURING THE NATIONAL ANTHEM. VIOLA-TORS WILL BE ESCORTED TO THE EXIT. The intern and I stopped. I placed my hand over my heart, and the little girl sang a heartbreakingly beautiful rendition of the song. At the last note, deafening fireworks exploded all over the stadium like we were being attacked by unseen enemy forces. When the smoke cleared, the flag had dis-appeared back into the rafters, and the podium and little girl were gone, replaced by Bubby, who was holding a coin in his little paw. The opposing team, the Atlanta Kudzus, wore beige body tights with strategically placed green leaves all over, like they were Eves who'd escaped from the Garden of Eden. They wore shiny gold helmets atop their heads that reflected the stadium lights. The Trash Bandits were out there, too. Bubby held the ceremonial coin in both his paws and, at the signal of the referee, who was the sole male human being on the field other than me, Bubby heaved the coin into the air over the heads of all those people and it softly bounced end over end on the green carpeting. HEADS, the announcer's voice boomed. ATLANTA WILL RECEIVE.

No, wait. There was another male human being on the field. It was the mascot for the Trash Pandas. According to the back of his t-shirt, his name was "STEVE." He was wearing flip-flops, cut-off shorts, mirrored sunglasses and a wild tangle of hair on his head. His beet-red and peeling skin told me he'd been in the sun too long. The front of his t-shirt announced him as #FLORIDAMAN. He pumped his fists. He capered around the margins of the field, setting things on fire.

I felt a soft touch on my elbow. It was the intern. "We need to get off the field, sir." She'd smeared her nose makeup. She seemed a bit disturbed. Upset.

"Are you okay?" I asked her.

"Follow me," she said.

I followed her.

We went through more tunnels, eventually finding an elevator. The intern swiped a card and the elevator came to life. The doors opened and I stepped inside. She stood outside of the elevator, looking at me with sad eyes. She was weeping.

"Are you okay?" I asked.

"Have a nice game," she said, her voice cracking, as she burst into tears.

The doors slid shut. I never saw her again.

So many people on this planet. So many lives that we know nothing about.

The thing about this country is that none of us are allowed to be sad. It's considered to be a toxic and pharmaceutically curable condition.

The elevator shot skyward. For a moment, I had a vision of shooting through the roof of the marshmallow stadium, Wonka style. Then the elevator came to a stop, the doors opened and I stepped into a luxury suite, where more women dressed as sexualized raccoons awaited me. LaShonda was also there, talking into her phone. She noticed me and waved me in while continuing her conversation. There were six women in the room to wait on the two of us.

TV sets hanging from the ceiling showed the action on the field. The furniture in the room was all mid-century modern, like we'd wandered onto the set of *The Dick Van Dyke Show*. There was beer in a giant container shaped like a beer can. I started to open up the container, but a raccoon woman quietly slipped over and said, "Allow me, sir." She extracted the beer, opened it, and poured it into a chilled glass from a refrigerator next to the giant beer can.

"Thank you," I said.

The elevator doors pinged open, and Bubby came galloping out. The raccoon women squealed with delight. He leapt upon the table with all the food on it, whipped off the metal lid from one tray, and immediately began gobbling down all the food in it with a sort of manic intensity. I think it was pulled pork.

"He didn't have breakfast this morning," I said.

"Oh," the woman manning the buffet table went.

"Also, he's a wild animal. I'd stay out of his way. He could bite you."

"Yes, sir," the woman manning the buffet table said, taking a half step back.

I heard cheering. I looked up at the TV set and watched as my seatmate from the limo threw a tight spiral 25 yards downfield to an open receiver, who ran for a touchdown. The stadium shook with explosions. I looked down at the field and saw a pirate ship on wheels rolling across the 50 yard line, firing cannons. Air raid sirens went off, too, because of course you'd fire up the air raid sirens for an 18th century pirate ship.

"What the hell does a pirate ship have to do with football-playing raccoons?" I asked aloud.

"What does anything have to do with anything?" one of the servers asked me with a wry smile. She had another can of beer at the ready and topped off my glass. "Let me know when that glass warms up. We have plenty more chilled in the fridge."

I heard a loud belch. Bubby was working on the second tray of food. I think it was nachos. He was making a mess.

We rode home without the accompaniment of the quarterback. She'd been sacked in the fourth quarter by an opposing linebacker whose jersey announced her as Bouncing Betty. The quarterback, whose name I never learned because I didn't want to know it, was taken to Tampa General across the bay. Something about a concussion protocol. Also, her knee had bent at a sickening angle.

LaShonda had spent the entire game on the phone, and the entire limo ride back to Sarasota on the phone. Bubby had gone from one metal serving tray to the next, gobbling down the contents. His little bucket hat was missing, and his t-shirt was shredded. Food bits were stuck all over his pelt and muzzle. He passed out in the limo, muttering to himself, "Fly, fly, fly."

The limo pulled up to my house. I'd started thinking of it as "my house" and not just the house that I grew up in, my grandparents' house. The house that formerly belonged to my grandparents. They were both gone, after all. Departed to the great beyond.

I scooped Bubby up in my arms and stepped out of the stretch Fiat. The street was strangely quiet. Nothing was left but the detritus from the raccoon festival. The sun was going down, turning the sky a blend of purple and orange and red. Just like the Tampa Bay Trash Bandit uniforms. So that's where they got it from. Hmph.

LaShonda rolled down her window, placing her hand over the phone. "I'll see you around, okay?"

"Okay. What's going on? Where is everybody?"

"The plane crash."

"Plane crash?"

"Haven't you heard?"

"No."

"There was a plane crash in Oneco. It was a jet flying in to Sarasota Bradenton International Airport from Belize. The plane crashed with one hundred passengers on board, burst into flames, and yet everyone survived."

"Oh."

"Once Sharma-LeenXXX, the sleepy-eyed star of Instagram, left, the whole crowd kind of followed her up to Oneco. Yahoo News is calling her a bad gal goddess."

"Because she's helping?"

"No, because the dress she's wearing shows a lot of her leg."

"She is helping though, right?"

"If by 'helping' you mean 'she's attracting a lot of attention to the plane crash' then you're right. She's taking selfies with survivors and first responders. She got everyone to light candles."

"I guess we can only do what we can do."

"Take care of yourself, Tris. You'd be a catch if you had one ounce of ambition." This is something a woman says when she likes a man, but isn't sexually attracted to him.

"I guess I'll never be a catch then."

Her window went up, and the limo rolled away.

I walked around back to the lanai and set Bubby in a lounge chair. He could spend the night outside. Maybe he'd run away, leave me alone. It was fun while it lasted.

I must have left the TV on, I figured. I could see the glow from it lighting up the living room. I walked back around to the front door and discovered that it had been forced open with a crowbar. I knew that because the crowbar had been tossed in the bushes next to the front door. I picked up the crowbar and held it like a club. I crept into my house.

My cousin Carwyn was sitting on the couch, dressed in a pea-green adult onesie. In white block letters on the front, like a billboard, NO FAT CHICKS.

"I'm free-balling," he told me.

"Thanks for the update, Carwyn." I lowered the crowbar, and then set it on the kitchen counter.

"So you recognize me?"

"How could I forget you? You tormented me every summer for ten years. You made me want to light a match and blow up Benzene Township, Pennsylvania once and for all."

"Heh, heh. That was some light ribbing, cousin Tris." He was surrounded by empties. He brushed some of them off the couch and onto the floor. "You're out of beer."

"No kidding."

"You want to know the truth? You look like shit."

"I wish people would stop telling me that. It might sink in."

"Where's that raccoon? I saw you with him on TV. I want him."

"Want him?"

"I want to eat him. Eat his heart, liver and brain. Then I'll possess his power."

"And what power is that?"

"I don't know. I was hoping you'd tell me."

"He's a talking, dancing raccoon. He's about as powerful as a fart in a windstorm. Go eat your congressman instead. I'm sure he'd taste better."

"So you don't have the raccoon anymore. That's what you're telling me."

"My God, you're perceptive. You hold down the fort. I'll go buy some more beer."

"You're all right, Tris. It don't matter that you killed my uncle good and dead, and the rest of your family. You're all right."

"Thanks. Think you could fix the door while I'm out?"

"Consider it done."

True to his word, by the time I got back from the Eckerd's with another 30 pack, Carwyn had fixed the door. I found him in his position on the couch, gnawing on a piece of Publix fried chicken. Welsh Wanderers have a bad reputation for charging double for half-assed repairs.

That's what I am. I'm a Welsh Wanderer. Or my father was.

I spent my summers as a child with the Edgar clan out in Pennsylvania during August, the month when the family rallied at our base of operations. My grandfather would drive me up from Florida and drop me off with Carwyn's family, and one of the Edgars would drive me back.

The other 11 months of the year, Edgars drove around the country in well-appointed pick-up trucks looking for easy pickings—elderly couples with missing shingles on their roofs, and the like. The craftier Edgars would sneak into houses and create problems, and then come by the next day to offer to fix them. While they were fixing the house, they'd steal the silverware, and so on.

"Where's your truck?"

"In your garage."

"How much have you stolen from the house so far?"

"Nothing. Jesus. Your grandparents were dirt poor."

"You check under the kitchen sink?"

"You know I did."

"Under the cabinet drawers?"

"I'm not an amateur."

"Dig up the backyard a bit?"

"Metal detector." He spat. "Nothing. There's nothing here. The wiring isn't even made of copper. Your TV barely works. I ain't even gonna charge you for fixing your door."

"Mighty nice of you."

"Hell, we're family. It's the least I could do."

I tossed him a beer out of the 30 pack, got one out for myself, and slid the rest of the beer into the fridge.

"The raccoon thing. That was a fake, right?"

"Yeah. They caught on to me though. That's why they all left."

"Thought them leaving had to do with that plane crash."

"That, too. Not much of an attention span in this country anymore."

We sipped silently on our beers for a while. I leaned against the kitchen counter, looking over at him. I found I didn't hate him anymore. I didn't hate anyone. I didn't love anyone either. I'd achieved a perfect level of numbness. Maybe it was all the beer. I'd had a lot at the game.

"You can ride along with me if you like. Could always use a sidekick. You talk all good and stuff, and I'm good at B and E. We'd could do a lot of crimes, not get caught."

"I'll think about it."

"Don't think too long. I'm leaving tomorrow."

I sat down on my grandfather's chair. I'd never sat in it before. It felt like it fit. "What are we watching?"

Carwyn turned on the set with the remote. "I've seen this one before," he said as the screen filled with another contest show. "This is a talent show with bands pretending to be other bands."

The show was called *Almost Live*. I recognized the people on the tube. It was my old band, Stop Making Cents, which was a Talking Heads cover band made up of people I'd worked with at Buy and Bye. They'd replaced me with someone who was a dead ringer for David Byrne. "The name of this song is 'The Book I Read,' and that's what it's about," my replacement said. The band tore into the song.

Behind him, Tina, the woman who'd talked me into joining the band, smiled and strummed on her bass. I was momentarily taken aback, but it quickly passed. I discovered I felt nothing other than a slight pang of recognition. There was no envy left inside. Just a void where all of that should have been. You could have measured all the shits I had left to give about Tina with a micrometer.

That's a lie. I lie a lot, mostly to myself. Lies keep me minimally functional. Freedom is not procured by a full enjoyment of what is desired, but by controlling the desire. I felt a slight rumble in my belly.

I got up. "I'll be right back."

"I'll be sitting here."

I walked into the master bedroom, and then quickly into the master bathroom. I vomited into the toilet, my eyes closed. It was all pouring out of me, every bit of it.

When I was done, I flipped on the light and looked into the toilet. It was red with blood.

TAKE INITIATIVE

I should tell you about the other woman in my second marriage. Actually, she was not the other woman because we didn't have sex. She was on my merchandising team at Buy and Bye. Let's call her "Tina Weymouth." She is a cautionary example of allowing someone into my life unbidden. Perhaps *the* cautionary example.

Tina is not her real name. It's the name of a bass player in a 1970's and '80's era band called Talking Heads. But let's call her Tina. I like that. It simplifies things. It makes it easier to talk about her.

The first thing Tina ever said to me that wasn't work-related was, "You look like shit."

"Thanks."

"Are you okay?" This is a deadly thing to say to someone needy and perpetually lonely like me, especially if you're a five-foot-nothing knockout. She was blonde, blue-eyed and curvy, like a fun-sized Diana Dors. I'd been ignoring her ever since she arrived on my team. It was my team, unfortunately. I'd been put in charge for some inexplicable reason, which, I'm going to guess, had something to do with having a college diploma. So it's not inexplicable. I'm certain that I didn't mention the degree the second time around at Buy and Bye, but the manager may have found it in my file from the first time around.

I said what I always said in answer to this question: "I'm fine." I could be on fire, my skin bubbling and peeling off my body and I'd say, "I'm fine."

"You have a sort of charm. But it's not charm. It's anti-charm." She said this while looking me square in the eye. "You don't seem happy." I lost myself in her gaze. When no one pays attention to you, that is freedom. Suddenly someone was paying attention to me. The wife had quickly turned a blind eye to everything that makes me who I am, instead concentrating on the parts that did not annoy her. Almost everything about me annoyed her. So she was paying as little attention to me as possible.

"It's no longer a crime in this country to not be happy. Perhaps that's contained in the 14th amendment. Or maybe there was a ruling by the Supreme Court—Marbury versus Go Fuck Yourself."

She laughed at that. She was freakishly undeterred. What was the sudden interest after the past few months of being ignored? I prefer being ignored. At least that's what I tell myself. "You want to get lunch?" Now she was asking me to lunch? "We can talk for a while."

I should have said, "Fuck no. Mind your own business." Instead I said, "Sure." There was a path here, a dangerous one, that I felt compelled to follow.

You see, there were two other workers who she'd also out-of-the-blue asked to lunch—Tim and Ricky.

After his lunch with Tina, Tim and Tina hung out together after work for a month. Tim became obsessed with her and nearly left his wife and four-year-old son for her. He ended up asking for a transfer and moved to South Carolina.

Ricky, who hit on every woman in the store, was also married. After he had his lunch with her, he became equally obsessed. He still worked in the same store, but had to be transferred to another merchandising team after sending Tina constant texts asking to see her considerable breasts.

Neither one of them had sex with her, but if you'd asked them, they would have said that they'd fallen head over heels in love with her. Like schoolboys. It's not love, I can tell you from first hand experience—it's infatuation. Infatuation is a one-way street.

Now it was my turn for lunch.

Why did I accept? Why did I go out to lunch with her, knowing what would happen? I've spent my life overanalyzing my life, so I have many answers for this. Here are the top eight answers for why I said yes to lunch. They are, necessarily, contradictory.

1. I was lonely. Bitterly so. Despite being married. Boo hoo.

2. I am self destructive, especially when it comes to interpersonal relationships. Having lunch with Tina was the equivalent of pouring diesel fuel over my head and then sticking a lit blowtorch in my ear.

3. I thought that I was immune to her charms, that my personal metaphysics kept me safe from anything like what Tina had on offer. I had logic on my side. "If Tina is a sufficient cause of heartache at Buy and Bye, then the presence of heartache at Buy and Bye implies the prior presence of Tina. The presence of Tina, however, does not imply that heartache will occur." I had an entire IF, THEN graph written in loopy cursive on the whiteboard of my consciousness. Hey, man: I wrote a book that was embraced by Norwegian philosophers, therefore I could think myself out of a problem that had occurred to non-philosophical-minded non-philosopher types like Tim and Ricky. And if thinking didn't keep me immune, I had my

trusty hip flask to blunt any errant brainwaves and/or hormonal challenges.

4. I wanted to feel something. Anything. I was numb. I am numb. I continue to be numb. Numbness is my thing. But sometimes numbness can be tiresome. How about some non-numbness? Sure. That. A vacation from NumbLand City, the capital of Numbsylvania. I am the Governor of Numbsylvania. Then, once I felt what ol' Tim and ol' Ricky felt, I'd bail, go back to ol' whatshername. The wife. LeeAnn. Yeah, her. And numbness.

5. No, wait. I wanted to destroy my already destroyed marriage, that I pretty much destroyed in advance of hanging out with a woman who looked like a two-thirds-sized Diana Dors circa 1958. Tina was a handy molotov cocktail. I'd see the effects firsthand. Boom. Marriage immolation.

6. It's all Tina's fault. I was helpless. I was a whiny little lamb led to the slaughter. Reason number six is bullshit.

7. I am a monster who wanted to feel sexy little Tina up. Reason number seven is, perhaps, not bullshit.

8. I was about to embark on an adventure, and, like most of my adventures, this one was not planned. It was improvisational, like most of my life. I am the man who leaps into a river without knowing the name of the river, or where it flows. Will I drown? Where will I wash up? Who knows? That's part of the adventure. One of these days, a person who wants me dead will hand me a bottle of strychnine and say, "Drink up!" and I will. *Mazel tov!* I will drink that bottle down to the bitter dregs, and as I'm clutching my chest, col-

lapsing to the faded and peeling linoleum flooring while blood squirts out of many of my favorite orifices, my last thought will be, "What's next?"

I could tell you which of these eight answers are valid—possibly all of them are valid—but now that you've listened this far, you go ahead and pick. Take a few minutes. Feel free to use the napkins from the donut table as scrap paper. There are no wrong answers.

Wait. There are plenty of wrong answers. Life is filled with wrong answers. Here's an example.

Tina: "You want to get lunch? We can talk for a while."

Wrong answer: "Sure."

Right answer: "I'm going to go drink my lunch from this handy hip flask alone and forget that we almost had a conversation. By the way, you're off my team. Go forth and hang with other Buy and Bye drones. Have a great Buy and Bye day."

I have only a vague recollection of what we talked about at lunch. I don't remember what I had for lunch. Did we eat? Pretty sure that we did. I remember that Tina hung on every word out of my mouth, like I was someone who mattered. Let's be clear: I've made it a lifestyle choice to be someone who doesn't matter in the least. But that doesn't mean that I don't want to be taken seriously on occasion, like someone who matters. Which I'm not.

I remember telling her that LeeAnn had saved my life, that without her I'd be dead. Or my liver would be dead, which would lead directly to my death. When LeeAnn was around, I felt no need to drink. LeeAnn made me regular person suppers when she was home. We engaged in regular person marital repartee. We had amazing sex. Look at us being married, I'd say to myself. Look at me being a husband who eats a roasted chicken that my wife prepared in an oven in our shared domicile. We are *so* married! So what if she's homely? Big deal. I'm no Johnny Depp. LeeAnn took pains to remind me of that nearly every day when she'd tweeze my ear hairs for me, or scratch my back, which is covered over in itchy moles.

I have a hypothesis that all of my moles will someday unite into one supermole on my back. At that point, I will shout, "The process is complete!"

"Have you ever been in a band?" Tina asked. "Because your voice reminds me of David Byrne's voice. His spoken word voice. Are you familiar with Talking Heads?"

I went to a liberal arts college and majored in philosophy. Of course I am familiar with Talking Heads. "No," I lied. "Who is that?"

That gave her the opportunity to lean over and touch my arm. "They are the greatest band in the universe." Her touch sent little jolts of electricity through me. I went all lightheaded. I hadn't felt like this since being molested by a waitress twice my age who eventually married and divorced me. Let us chant her name: *Delores! Delores! Delores!*

Did Tina know what she was doing? Yes. *No.* Maybe. She was beautiful, but approachable—an intoxicating combination. She was built like a 13-year-old boy's wet dream. But did she know what she was doing? Was it inadvertent? And would it make a difference if she did know the effect that she had on people like me, Tim and Ricky?

Now I was lumping myself in with Tim and Ricky. Me! A guy who could talk about Immanuel Kant like I'd met the cocksucker.

What does her intent count for in this situation? Even if she was seducing me, what did it matter? Her intent does not matter. The only thing you can control in this life is yourself. All else is beyond control. To say that you're helpless in the presence of another is to lie to yourself. I wanted to be near her. I wanted her attention. Blame that on me, not on her.

She pulled her iPod out of her back pocket and plugged in her headphones. She cued up, "Uh Oh, Love Comes to Town." She reached over and placed the earphones into my ears and hit play. She stared into my eyes while the song played, coaxing smiles out of me. When it was over, she extracted the earphones. Her fingertips grazed my ears from whence a few hours earlier, LeeAnn had yanked out tiny hairs with a pair of tweezers. "What do you think?"

"Okay."

"Just okay?"

"Yes, they're great. Talking Heads."

"So I'm forming a cover band with a couple of guys from work. Do you think you could sing like that? How long do you think it would take you to memorize some lyrics?"

"Me?"

"Sure. You're just like him. You're like a real-life David Byrne."

"There's already a real-life David Byrne."

"Then you're a realistic substitute. We'll have to get you a wig. I know someone who works at the Lyric Opera. We could get you one. Then we need to get you a big suit."

"You make it sound like I've already agreed to this."

She touched my hand and made eye contact again. "Haven't you?"

Tina arranged for us to practice at the Buy and Bye in the warehouse after our shift. The other two men in the band, let's call them Jerry (guitar) and Chris (drums), were also clearly enamored with her. During breaks, when she would go off to the bathroom to freshen up, we'd have arguments about which one of us was her best friend.

She overheard us one time and informed us that we were all her "dear friends." This was unsatisfying news for me, and for Jerry, and for Chris.

None of us were destined to be her paramour. That fate belonged to Dagger, her six-foot-nine boyfriend who played Lemmy in a Motörhead tribute band. Dagger would come to our practice sessions on occasion to slouch in a gaming chair that had been pulled off the sales floor because it listed to starboard. He would make unkind comments. The two of them would fight in front of us, giving the three male bandmates unreasonable expectations about our prospects with her. Then the two of them would make up a few nights later, dashing our hopes. He called her, "Babe." She called him, "Babe."

After practice one night, she invited me out to the Bucktown Diner, an all-night restaurant that served vegan knockoffs of actual food. There was "meatloaf" and "burgers" and "macaroni and cheese," which looked like actual food and tasted like cardboard. It was just the two of us. She told me I was her best friend, not like the others who sent her mash notes. She told stories of other men who'd been her best friends, who'd confessed their love for her and ruined everything. Not like me. I'd never sent her a mash note, never confessed my love.

"Do you want me to send you something like that?"

"We don't have that kind of relationship. Our relationship is pure."

"Okay."

She gave me that intense eye contact again, and her undivided attention. It was like being in a spotlight on a stage in the moment before thunderous applause begins. Heady. Blinding.

Then she dropped the bomb that Dagger had fathered a daughter with a groupie and that Dagger and the groupie were going to run off to New York and get hitched.

I was angry at Dagger. How dare he break her heart! "That sucks," I said.

"He's the love of my life."

My darkest thoughts had her marrying Dagger, and then Dagger would somehow kill her. No, wait. My darkest thoughts had me leaving LeeAnn, marrying Tina, and then I accidentally kill her, maybe in a car. But the dark thoughts about Dagger were more prevalent.

"Fuck him. He's younger than I am. He'll come around, eventually." Tina talked for a while about how she met Dagger. He was the bouncer at a bar where she wore a magician's assistant uniform and served drinks out of shot glasses that she carried around on the brim of a top hat. After all the shot glasses were gone, she'd lift up the hat and a dove would fly out.

She'd also gone to college, but had dropped out a few credits shy of a bachelor's degree in electrical engineering at Georgia Tech.

She had permanent wanderlust. She drove a Chevy Citation eaten through with rust that she repaired constantly. There's something about a woman who can fix things, who can will her way through life, that appeals greatly to me. Maybe it's because I'm so completely useless. Tina could have used her beauty to lean on men, but she didn't. She made her own way. I admired her.

She went on and on about Dagger. I didn't want to hear it anymore. Tina sensed it and drove me home in the rusty Citation. As the car pulled up to the curb, I asked her if I could kiss her on the cheek. She allowed it. Electricity!

I trudged up the stairs of the apartment building. LeeAnn was waiting for me at the top in a frumpy University of Illinois night shirt. There was a giant, faded orange "I" in the middle of her chest. "Out with your girlfriend all night?"

"Band practice went long."

"Oh yeah?"

"Tina and Dagger broke up."

"You think it's permanent?"

"I doubt it. I think they'll get married, and he'll get drunk and beat her to death some night."

"Sounds like something you'd think. You want a beer?"

"I'm home with you. I don't want anything."

We went to bed. During our marriage, LeeAnn kept trading in our current pillow-top bed on a larger model. The latest bed was a California king. It felt like I was sleeping a continent away from her.

I needed closeness that night. I wanted to wrap my arms around LeeAnn's warm body. I wanted her to wrap her arms around me. I wanted her to acknowledge me as a necessary part of her life. I wanted to ask her to be a necessary part of mine. I didn't know how to ask for such things, and we'd never done anything that before. We were roomies with benefits who happened to be married.

After she clicked off the bedside lamp, I low-crawled my way across the ocean-liner of a bed, and upon arrival on LeeAnn's side, she said coldly, "Are you trying to get with me?"

I had no answer for that. I said nothing and retreated.

As I drifted off to sleep, I remembered Tina's eyes looking at me. I was a person in her eyes. I was real. Maybe this band shit would turn out. Maybe I would, despite every impulse I'd had since I was six years old, become a respected member of society, one of the visible people instead of the invisible.

The band shit worked out for a while. We got regular gigs at a hipster bowling alley on the near Northside. We worked various streetfests throughout the city. We opened for a Blondie tribute band at Northbrook Fest. We opened for a Ramones tribute band at the Lincoln Avenue Bratwurst Fest.

LeeAnn kicked me out. I couch-surfed. I even stayed at Tina's place for a week. It was during that week, after we sat talking all night, that I asked Tina to be my girlfriend. "I know that I'm older than you, that I've lost my hair. But I have a feeling that I'll live to a ripe old age. And we have a connection, you know. I feel that."

"I've had a connection with a lot of people," she said, looking away from me. I felt a coldness kick in. I'd crossed the uncrossable line.

The spotlight suddenly clicked off. I was alone on the stage. The audience lights came up. There was no one left in the seats. I understood.

And my heart. My heart hurt so much. I missed Lee-Ann in that moment. I'd fucked up. This time it was permanent.

But I understood who was responsible for my heart hurting. It was me. I'd done this to myself. Hope is toxic.

"Mind if I have a beer?" I asked her.

"I'm going to bed." She stood up, walked to her bedroom, and I heard the door shut, and then the lock click.

I sat in her living room drinking beer after beer. I drank all her beer. Before she got up the next morning, I got my shit together and left. I'd done this to myself.

We opened for a Motörhead tribute band at Wicker Park Fest. That's where Tina rediscovered the love of her life, Dagger, who hadn't married the groupie as it turned out. There wasn't even a baby. The two of them embraced after our set. Dagger took a knee and asked her to marry him, right there on stage. She said yes.

And my heart. My heart hurt so much. I'd done this to myself.

We look around for others to blame for our internal pain, but there is only one person it belongs to: the one who made it. No one outside of you makes your pain. You make it yourself, like a school project. Like an ugly, misshapen ashtray for grandpa in an arts and crafts class.

Speaking of which, I wrote Tina a florid letter thanking her for her friendship. I added to that an art project that could have been done by a minimally talented fourth grader—a crude painting of her with vintage Talking Heads buttons glued to the frame. I spent a week writing and rewriting and editing and rewriting the letter and a month on the art project. If I had to guess, she probably looked at it each item for approximately a minute, and then either tossed them into a drawer or into the closest dumpster. At least that's what I would have done with them.

Add that on top of my busted-up marriage, and I'd doubled my pain, doubled my fun.

I had that taste in my mouth. It was like burnt chocolate pudding scraped out of an old tin pot. I'd burnt the pudding. I was forcing myself to eat it.

I went to my divorce proceedings a few weeks later. There was LeeAnn. There was the end of marriage. There was the end of doing such things to myself.

Before Carwyn departed, he attempted to bond with me. "Had a great floater the other day that was at the top of my vision," he said over his breakfast beer. "My mind kept seeing it as 'being attacked by bird,' so I ducked. Repeatedly. All day."

"Uh huh."

He said that his sole ambition these days is to devolve into lassitude. He finished off the beer. He crushed the can against his forehead. "It's my curse to have the unfortunate drive to work. Sure you don't want to tag along? I feel bad about leaving you in this dump."

"I'll figure something out. I always do."

"It's the Edgar way."

"The Edgar way," I repeated. I chuckled a bit. Then I laughed out loud. "The Edgar way? Oh my God, yes."

Should I tell you my first memory of Carwyn? It'll change the way you look at me. Or maybe it won't. It'll definitely change the way you look at Carwyn.

The Edgar family was originally from Wales. We were Romany, I'm told. Welsh Wanderers. This explained my father's love of driving, of packing up the Ford and taking off on the open road as a traveling salesman.

This was the year before I killed my family, when I was five. I'd wandered away from the family compound, all those pickup trucks and station wagons parked in circles, all those tents. I'd decided to go for a walk in the woods. There was always a faint whiff of petroleum in the air there, to go along with scent of towering eastern hemlocks.

I heard Carwyn crying before I saw him. He was much bigger than me then, just as he is today.

He had four older brothers. The one who was with him was the oldest, Griffith, who was in his teens at that point. Griffith could have played linebacker for the Benzene High School Oilers, if he had gone to school. But, like a lot of people in my family, he preferred what he called "the School of Hard Knocks," that is, learning only from his own limited experience and not benefitting from the experiences of others. He was tall and blonde, muscled. He wore unbending workman's clothes, like almost every male in the family.

I found Griffith standing over Carwyn. Griffith was zipping up his Dickies jeans. Carwyn was still bent face-down over a tree stump. He was not crying anymore. His face was stone cold. He'd gone deep inside himself, disappeared. "Get dressed, you pussy," Griffith said.

I'd frozen on the dirt path I was on. I could hear blackbirds cawing somewhere.

Carwyn noticed me first. "Hey!" he went, pulling up his pants. "Hey!"

Griffith turned and stared at me. At first, he looked a little panicked. But like all Edgars, when caught, he turned the tables quickly. "You think you saw something? Huh, cousin Tristram? You think you saw something, you little shit? Think you can make money off it?" He was big, but quick. I tried to run, but he was on me before I could take three steps. He hoisted me up onto his shoulder, like a bag of sakrete, and then set me down in front of Carwyn, who'd zipped up by this time. He had on a Transformers t-shirt. Robots in disguise. "What should we do with him?"

"Dunno," Carwyn went.

"You don't know much, do you? He's gonna tell, and then everyone'll know you're a faggot, won't they?"

Carwyn panicked a bit and stared at me. What he saw in my eyes made him angry. I pitied him.

"I won't tell," I said.

"He won't tell," Griffith said. "Did you hear him? He won't tell. Tell what, big mouth? What won't you tell?"

"Nothing," I said, looking from the big one to the much bigger one and then back again. "Nothing to tell." When my gaze returned to Carwyn, I saw that he was enraged.

"You're the faggot!" he shouted. He hopped to his feet. "Stand up!" I stood up. He knocked me down. "Stand up!" I stood up. He knocked me down again. This went on a few more times.

We all heard my mother calling out my name. "Tristram! Tristram!"

Griffith knelt down and pointed in my face. I can remember every pockmark on his face. His breath smelled like rotten eggs. "Whatever you think you saw? You didn't."

Carwyn sneered. "Faggot." He pushed me down one last time, and then the two of them ran off together, laughing.

My mother found me. I was dirty. "What have you been doing?" She tried brushing me off with her hands. "I should have had more girls."

When I remember this, I cannot I remember her face. It all becomes blurry at that point. I can remember everything, every detail, about my two cousins, but my mother is indistinct.

I remember her bringing me back to the campsite, and my father going through his usual rages at me. That's what I remember about him—the shouting. I don't remember his face either.

My brother and sister? I don't know. Ghosts.

God knows I've tried to remember them all, but there's nothing there. Vapor. Maybe that's for the best.

Carwyn spent the rest of that trip finding me when I was vulnerable and alone, and knocking me over. He was physically superior to me. That point was made. I didn't forget that.

So the next year, when it came time to go back to Pennsylvania, I begged to stay with my grandparents. My father pointed out to me that I was six and had no choice in the matter. As it turned out, I did have some say.

The irony was that the next ten times I went up to Pennsylvania, dropped off by my well-meaning grandfather, I was all alone. I was vulnerable the whole time. Carwyn figured out what he could do to me. It was mostly beatings, though one time he tried to electrocute me with a toaster while I was in a makeshift outdoor shower. I shrieked a bit, until I realized the toaster wasn't plugged in.

No, he didn't try to bugger me. To his credit, that was a line he didn't cross.

He probably wouldn't have administered all those beatings, I think, if I didn't keep looking at him in the same way. He took the hate. He welcomed it, I think. But not the pity that rode shotgun alongside it.

Twenty years after the last time I saw him, both of us men on standing on the periphery of middle age, I could finally look at him without pity and without hate. I saw a man, like any other man, bearing the scars of his life, doing the best he could. He turned out to be a better man than I am, despite being a scam artist.

He had a wife and two teenaged daughters. The way he talked about his family, I could tell he doted on them.

I told him I envied him. I did envy him. I do.

He smiled broadly. "Goodbye, Tris," he said, getting into his pickup truck. "Sorry about... I dunno. Everything?" There was this look in his eyes. People in general have lowered expectations for me that I fail to exceed.

He was right about pity. It didn't feel great.

I spent much of the day fixing my grandparents' room. It involved large amounts of wall plaster and, eventually, paint. I painted the whole room with the remains of half-empty cans of paint I'd found in the garage that I dumped in one PVC bucket. I'd neglected to cover the shredded carpet, so there were gloops of paint and plaster stuck in random spots, forming a crust on the shredded shag. It was cheaper than paying someone, I guess.

I did all my work in silence, not worrying about my roommate, or former roommate. I didn't care where he was. I hoped he'd wandered off.

Under the bed, while I was vacuuming up various bits of detritus that had collected there—including mattress stuffing, paint chips, carpet bits and chunks of gypsum—I found the collar that Bubby had on when I'd first made his acquaintance less than a week before. I turned off the vacuum and twisted the collar around in my hands. I read the dog tag attached to it:

NAVAIR

ORLANDO FL

SUBJ #407

On the obverse side was a crest emblazoned with pilot's wings and three stars. I set it down on the bureau.

I took the PVC bucket and used paint brushes out to the nearly empty garage and left them there. I wasn't going to clean them. I stripped off my paint spattered clothes and shoved them in the bucket, too.

I took a shower and then put on my grandfather's clothes. The clothes fit, and they felt right—blue, short-sleeved work shirt, black dungarees, moth-eaten boxer shorts, padded socks, sparkless work shoes. "Dead man's clothes," I muttered to myself.

I still had the salty, metallic taste of blood in my mouth. I checked out my eyes in the bathroom mirror. They were bloodshot, but no signs of jaundice. Not yet anyway. I wasn't worried, really. More like mildly interested in my progress. It's hard work being an alcoholic. You have to drink every day, no matter what. It takes commitment.

I found my iPad and checked my email, standing in the kitchen. There were 200 emails in there. After I deleted all the Canadian Viagra offers, I was down to 120 emails.

One of the emails was from Harry Lunte, Agent Extraordinaire: "Idea! We have you two star in a touring production of *Wayne's World The Musical*. Bandit will be Wayne and you'll be Garth. It's money!" I deleted it.

Another email was from a self-styled naturalist named Dr. Pinch Thomas, who was the author of a book titled, *Geese: Nature's Jerks*, according to the CV he'd helpfully attached to the email. "Given your permission, of course, I should like to test the specimen to find out if it can, indeed, speak, or if it is merely imitating sounds that resemble speech. If the specimen can, in fact, speak, I should like permission to dissect it, humanely of course, and extract its brain so as to study the speech centers. I have performed this with geese. Said geese have bitten me and my lab assistants and have uttered the most profane language imaginable in their own dark tongue." He signed off with, "I remain your humble servant..." I deleted it.

A man who was clearly a schizophrenic accused Bubby of breaking into his house and moving things around. "A week ago, I woke up around midnight, opened my bedroom door and the entire living room/kitchen area was filled with raccoon spoor. I panicked a bit, knowing that a particularly clever raccoon had managed to get into the apartment, so I turned on the lights and peered around. I thought that maybe one of my neighbors had left open the front door of the apartment building, so I went downstairs. Nope. By the time I made it back to my apartment, the stench was gone, so the culprit, who I shall assume is your raccoon, he being more clever than most raccoons, had made his getaway while I crept around the interior stairs near my mailbox, checking for footprints. I went back to bed for a couple of hours of restless near-sleep and then gave up and got up. I am writing you now with the intent of exposing your raccoon's nefarious schemes against me. Number one: He clearly opened my wallet, read my date of birth, Social Security number, and other private information, and then used said information to enroll me in the Legume of the Month Club. The first shipment arrived today. I am allergic to peas. Your raccoon knows this, having read my first alert card, also in my wallet." Etc. I deleted the email.

Several emails accused me of "being gay with the raccoon." I couldn't tell if they were more offended by the bestiality or the homosexuality. I deleted them.

One emailer, who was an inmate at a minimum security prison in Arcadia, Florida, wrote, "Hey, sexy! Saw you on TV. Mmm, mmm! That's the way I like my men! Bald, bad, drunk and on TV!!! I can't wait to get out of this place and come find you. Kisses!!!" She offered to do unspeakable things to me in front of the raccoon because she liked it when animals watched her have sex, especially with a sweaty bald guy. She enclosed a photo of herself pre-incarceration. I recognized the look in her eyes. I'd worked with women like her before. They stole out of the till. They shoved product in their underwear to sneak it out of the restaurant or store. I did not delete the email. I did not respond to it either. I was saving it for later, for when I was good and drunk.

There was an email from my old publisher, Timothy Murchison. "YOU SHOULD WRITE A MEMOIR ABOUT THE RACCOON LETS GET TOGETHER AND DISCUSS THIS. BIG CHECK FOR YOU IF YOU AGREE SENDING A NEW CONTRACT FOR YOUR PURSUAL." I think he meant for my "perusal." Whatever. I deleted the email.

There was an email from Tina. "I know, according that letter that you wrote me, that you don't think we were really friends. How did you put it? Friends of convenience? What the fuck is that? I want you to know that I will always consider you a dear friend, no matter what you think. Don't worry. I'm not going to blow your deal with the raccoon (it's all fake, right?), or go on TV and tell everyone that you hit on me like a skeevy pervert, even though I could. The band was on TV recently... Did you see it? Dane is a nice guy, but he's not as good a David Byrne as you were." This was a lie. "Anyways, we could use the publicity if you'll let us play at your main stage. I hear it's a great scene there in Sarasota." It was both friendly and vaguely threatening. I'd hoped that I would quickly fade from her memory, and she would fade from mine. But that's the magic of an internet-connected world, I suppose. We're never allowed to forget anything.

I felt my heart race thinking about her, and felt the rush of blood into my head, and that feeling that my head might pop like a balloon. I remembered the way she paid attention to me, the way she treated me like I was someone worth knowing and my heart raced some more. "Stop it! Stop it!" I shouted at myself. We are what we repeatedly do. I am a shithead. I attempted to reason with myself, to use my dulled and atrophied intellect to fight back against that part of myself that is beyond reason.

"We are not troubled by things, but by the opinion that we have of things," I said aloud.

"The supreme function of reason is to show man that some things are beyond reason," I replied.

I deleted the email and emptied the little trash can so I wouldn't go and pull the email out of there and write her back once I got good and drunk.

I opened the refrigerator and saw that Carwyn had made off with the rest of the beer. I panicked a bit. I needed a drink right away—*rapidement, vivement, sans délai*. I scurried to my bathroom and found a plastic bottle of gin hidden under the sink in there and upended it into my throat. I felt that momentary relief. I saw myself in the mirror. I seemed to be aging while I watched.

I found my phone and used the BoozNow app to order another case of cheap beer and a handle of Jack Daniel's. I should have been doing this all along, but my thinking was that the walk to the Eckerd's would do me good. Now I wasn't interested in doing myself any favors. The phone chimed back that the booze would be delivered within 30 minutes.

"Okay," I said, panic subsiding. "Good job."

I gave myself a pep talk. "This is all within you. All of this. There is nothing external that can touch you, other than a sword or a gun. In a little while, you will forget everything. In a little while, everything will forget you. We suffer more in imagination than in reality." And so on. There are a lot of aphorisms to chew on when the booze runs out.

I paced for a while.

I missed the raccoon and all the attention. The whole ruckus was diverting. It kept me from assaulting myself from within.

I felt a familiar gurgle from my guts that quickly bubbled up my throat and into my mouth. I ran to the bathroom. I vomited up the gin and about a half pint of blood into the toilet. I spat. I turned on the tap in the sink, cupped my hands underneath it, slurped out of my hands, and swished the rotten egg scented water around my mouth. I spat. I threw up again, this time in the sink. I flushed the toilet, but blood spatters remained in the bowl and around the rim. I'd wipe up the sink and toilet later, I promised myself.

The doorbell rang. I sprinted to the door and flung it open. It was the delivery guy. I recognized him from about a week before at the Eckerd's. He wasn't wearing his Freaky Frank's uniform this time, but it was the same guy.

"Jesus," he said.

"Pardon?"

"You look like shit."

"Thanks." I took the case of beer out of his hands and set it on the floor inside. He handed me the bottle of Jack Daniel's, and I set that beside the beer. "Here," I said, handing him a twenty.

"You already paid with the app."

"It's a tip."

"You already tipped me with the app."

"Just take it."

"Big shot, huh? You got blood all over your lips, big shot. Your chin, too."

"I know that. You don't think I know that? I know that." If my time in the service industry taught me anything, it's how awful people can be if they believe themselves to be superior to you. I'm sure that he'd been shat on approximately a million times by people ordering sandwiches or booze. I wanted to be nice, but he wasn't letting me. "You want the tip or not?"

He snatched the twenty out of my hand. "Fuck you, big shot." He stalked out to an idling, rust-eaten F-150 and got in. Then he drove up on my lawn and did a donut, leaving gigantic ruts behind. He leaned out the driver's side window and flipped me off, then ran over my mailbox driving away.

I closed the front door. I felt a little lightheaded. Blood loss? I snatched up the bourbon and took it back to the kitchen with me. I found Pop's old coffee cup in the cupboard, bright red with a yellow hammer and sickle, and filled it with some Jack. I took a sip and it burned like fire going down.

"Let's answer a few more emails before complete liver shutdown, shall we?" I said aloud. "Good plan!" I situated my iPad next to the coffee cup and soldiered on.

I opened an email from Big Ass Ron, who was the bouncer on *The Guy Morton Show*. As it turned out, he was also in charge of booking. "Hey! Big Ass Ron here! Just wanted to gage your interest in coming on The Show. We can devote a show to just you and Bubby. I like Bubby's style! He's a happening little fucker! Hit me back if you're interested."

I wrote: "Dear Big Ass Ron, Get fucked. Love, Bubby."

Then I wrote a second email: "Big Ass Ron! Sorry about that! Bubby got ahold of my computer. I had no idea he could spell, too. He's a mean little raccoon. I caught him peeing in my Corn Flakes this morning. Yours in Christ, Tris Edgar."

I opened an email from my second ex-wife. I took a long drink—felt the burn, embraced the burn, go burn go —and read: "I am worried about you. You did not look good on TV. I wish you would take better care of yourself, but I know that you won't. We didn't always get along, but that doesn't mean I wished you'd drink yourself to death. I'm sorry I didn't believe you about the drinking at the time. Please, Tris, check yourself into a facility. I know you don't want to hear this from me, but I'm begging you to get help."

My heart raced and raced. I took another drink. Burn. *Burn!* I typed: "Thanks for your concern. I'm fine." I hit send. I deleted her email.

I refilled my coffee cup and drank about half. It wasn't helping. Too many emails at once.

I heard a knock on the sliding glass door. I walked over and opened it. Bubby came in, dripping wet and scented with chlorine.

"Found the neighbor's pool, huh? How's it going?" I asked him.

"Feh," he went. He climbed up to the counter and drank out of the communist coffee cup.

"You hanging around now? Or are you gonna take off?" I asked him.

"Fly," he went. "Fly!"

Maybe he wasn't forming words. Maybe I was dreaming all of this. Maybe the whole thing was some sort of alcohol-poisoning-related hallucination.

Bubby polished off the whiskey in the cup and headed off to the bedroom.

I checked up on him ten minutes later and found him crashed out on the bed, sawing logs. I went back to the kitchen and typed "NAVAIR Orlando" into google and a Navy website immediately popped up. I clicked on the link and it took me to a page with a portrait of a pinch-faced woman in a Navy uniform glaring into the camera, an American flag behind her. CAPT AUDREY NOVAK, M.ENG., PH.D, USN, DIRECTOR OF RESEARCH.

I clicked on "contact," and a phone number came up. I called the number and was surprised that Captain Novak herself picked up. "Novak," she barked out matter-of-factly.

"Are you missing a raccoon?"

"Who is this?"

"A guy with a talking raccoon. We were on the news recently. Me and the raccoon."

"The news is of no interest to me," she snapped.

"Subject number four-oh-seven."

Her voice softened a smidge. "That little rascal made his escape about two weeks ago. Been looking for him."

"I'll give you my address." I did so. I told her a bit about how I'd found him and what had transpired.

She whistled appreciatively. "He must have hitched a ride with someone to make it that far. Says his name is 'Bubby Muck,' and likes to fly, huh? That's hilarious."

"Why's that?"

"Because my husband is Commander Bobby McCrae. He's an aviator. I'll be down there tomorrow. Keep that little jerk occupied. The government will compensate you handsomely. Plus, think of it as your patriotic duty. National security and all that."

"Sure."

"Thanks for calling Mister Edgar. See you tomorrow at about thirteen hundred." She hung up.

ASSUME NOTHING, QUESTION EVERYTHING

I still didn't have a permanent place to live in Chicago, post-divorce. I'd discovered a weekly rental place. It was a fully furnished efficiency apartment that didn't require a lease agreement, just an upfront payment each Friday for the following week. At $200 a week, it wasn't a bad deal. And it came with complimentary cable, water and power. They even washed my sheets for me. The neighbors could be a bit loud, but they usually didn't stay very long. The building, a beige cinderblock fortress, was alongside the Dan Ryan expressway. I could see my ex-wife's attorney lounging on her billboard from my window, and listen to the roar of the interstate.

I added 60 minutes on my phone at Buy and Bye, came home from work and called up my commie granddad, my drapes open, staring at Mary Jo Kowalski on her bill-board, bigger than life on a bearskin rug, blonde haired, wearing a pink satin teddy. The A/C must have been turned all the way up in the photographer's studio, or someone had rubbed a little ice on her nipples.

"Who's this?" is the way Pop answered the phone.

"Tris," I said.

"Who?"

"Your grandson. Tris."

"You don't have to yell."

"Clearly, I do."

"When are you coming home?"

"I have a home?"

"I said, 'When are you coming home?'"

"I heard you."

"You didn't answer me."

"I don't have any money. I can't come home."

"I'll pay for your ticket." He meant a bus ticket. Pop didn't believe in flying. It was a rich man's means of conveyance. Prols rolled.

"You'll pay for my ticket."

"That's what I said."

"Why?"

"Your grandmother is dying."

"She's been dying for half my life."

"She's serious this time. When can you come?"

"You expect me to pull up stakes and head down to Florida right now?"

"As soon as you can manage, yes."

"Why?"

"Why should I be the only one taking care of her?"

"Because you married her. Because she's your wife."

"Beyond that. Why?"

I sighed out loud. "What are you saying? Are you saying you want me to come live with you again?"

"I never wanted you to leave. It gets lonely, okay?"

"So you want me to come down there to keep you company?"

"Yes. Come down here to Florida and keep me company."

"Fine."

"Ah. Good. Go to the Trailways station tomorrow. There will be a ticket waiting for you there."

"Okay."

He hung up. For someone who claimed to miss me, he didn't seem to relish conversing with me.

I called up Buy and Bye and asked to speak to the manager, who by that time was an ill-tempered Pakistani man named Roger. I'd spoken to Roger twice, and both times he pointed out to me that in his country, he'd been a physician. Here, he was reduced to being in charge of slackers, miscreants and alcoholics. "I am living the American dream," he'd tell anyone listening. No one listened. We're a nation of talkers, not listeners.

"Hello, this is Roger. How may I help you, sir?"

"I quit, effective immediately."

"Which one is this?"

"Tristram Edgar. I'm in charge of Merchandising Team B."

"Have we spoken before, Mister Edgar?"

"No," I lied.

"That was my mistake, then. May I ask why you are leaving me shorthanded?"

"My grandmother is dying and I have to move back to Florida."

"Ah. I am very sorry to hear that. You have my condolences."

"Thanks."

He coughed, hacking up something whose shape and texture I could intuit over the phone. He spat. He must have been in the warehouse, or outside. "Wait a minute. We have spoken before, Mister Edgar. I remember you now. Are you sure you are not drunk at this moment? Perhaps you will regret quitting and making up a lie."

"I'm not drunk yet. And this is not a lie."

"You realize that you will never work at Buy and Bye again, do you not?"

"It's a sacrifice I'm willing to make." I told him where to mail the check.

"Goodbye, Mister Edgar."

"So long, doctor."

I drank the evening away, staring at the comely attorney on the billboard. I tried to masturbate and failed.

The following morning, I took a shower and put everything I owned into a large backpack that I'd stolen from Buy and Bye. There was room to spare in there. I checked out at the front desk, handed them my key. It wasn't much of a walk to the bus station. I lived in that part of town. The fall was just beginning to take hold, but not enough so that I needed a jacket. True to his word, Pop had purchased a one-way ticket to Sarasota. I showed the clerk my expired state of Illinois driver's license, which still had LeeAnn's address on it. The clerk handed me my ticket and I waited two hours to board the bus.

From Chicago to Atlanta, I sat next to Fitch Malpaso, a pop-eyed, mostly bald, toothless former minor league catcher on his way to coach at a minicamp for aspiring major league catchers. He long before spent up whatever pittance baseball had paid him and was happy for the pittance that he was going to be paid at the camp. He was eager to tell me stories about other bus trips he'd been on, playing for and against teams all over the country—Biscuits, Mudhens, Mudcats, Railsplitters, Skysox, Boardbusters, and so on. I learned more about minor league baseball over the course of 24 hours than I had in a lifetime of barely knowing that it existed. Most of his stories were not fascinating in the least, but his delivery was. He licked his lips before each story, winking with his protruding eye, smiling coquettishly. A slight whistle emitted from his nasal passages as he narrated his life. He wanted, desperately, to be interesting, especially to someone who wasn't a sports fan. It was his desperation I was interested in. The stories were mostly secondary. I perked up during his story about impregnating a fan when he was in rookie ball and her father chasing him down the street wielding one of Fitch's own bats, eventually breaking the bat over Fitch's radioulnar joint, which also broke. "Ruined my batting stroke," he said, wistfully. "Didn't care about the bat. It wasn't my gamer."

"What about the baby?"

"What baby?"

"The baby you had with the fan."

"Oh. I don't know. Aborted?"

"So there might be a little Malpaso wandering around out there."

"Who knows? Wouldn't be so little anymore. Shit, how long ago was all that? Eighteen years? Yeah. It's been eighteen years." He whistled at the elapsed time like it was a pretty girl wandering past a construction site. "Eighteen years in the minors."

In Atlanta, I changed buses, and sat next to a sly Afghan War soldier named Sergeant Malevich, who was wearing a baggy set of camouflage work clothes with matching brown suede boots. He was missing most of the pinkie finger on his right hand.

"They let you stay in the military without a pinkie finger?"

"Sure. Why not? Ain't my trigger pulling finger, is it?" He told me how he'd lost the finger while jogging. He was in Bagram Air Force Base. "Minding my own fucking business. Getting my pee-tee in. I hear a pop, and next thing I knew, my hand sprung a gusher. Goddamnedest thing I ever seen. And me, a seventy-one lima! Inside the wire! A career fobbit! Got me a purple heart, though.

That's all right. Lotsa promotion points for one of those bad boys. Made e-six."

I had no idea what he was talking about, so I nodded a lot, and then thanked him for his service, which seemed to irritate him.

He continued speaking in military gibberish for a while. Mostly his soliloquy was a primer on how to "get over" and "eating cheese" and "shamming," all of which had meaning for him, and none for me. I smiled and nodded, and then drifted off to sleep.

I woke up at dawn as the bus pulled into the Trailways bus depot in Sarasota. I blinked and yawned. My seatmate had departed sometime during the night. I got off the bus, and the driver handed me my mostly empty backpack from the luggage compartment.

My grandfather was not in evidence, so I walked over to a green Ford LTD cab idling at the curb and got in. My old high school acquaintance was at the wheel, and he recognized me instantly. "Dude! You're back!"

"I'm back."

"Heading to your grandparents' house?"

"I am. What happened to your other cab?"

"Caught fire. Or someone set it on fire. Totally bummed me out. So I bought this one used from Quick-E-Cab. Only had one-hundred-and-fifty-seven thousand miles on it."

"Practically new."

"Has a weird smell to it. I think a cat died in here. Or some sort of animal. That's why I keep the windows open. Also, the air conditioning doesn't work. Remember that time in band when the rat died underneath the practice space, like in an air duct or something? That smell, dude.

It didn't go away for a month. Man, I thought you were gonna throw up that whole month. You kept going, 'Bring out your dead! Bring out your dead!' Like all Monty Python and shit."

"How could I forget?" I handed him a twenty. "Say hello to my little friend, Andrew Jackson. Let's go."

He snatched the twenty out of my hand. "Andrew Jackson was a war criminal, dude. Killed, like, the Indians and shit."

"That he did. Let's go."

"So you shouldn't call him your friend, okay?"

"Noted. Let's go."

He was sulky all the way to the grandparents' house, and we didn't engage in any more banter, which was fine by me. I hadn't had a drink since Chicago. My nerves were tingling. I could hear a faint sound coming from the core of my brain, emanating from somewhere in the vicinity of the gyrus cinguli. It was like a rusty door hinge, squealing continually. It was the old, familiar keening that had kept me company since I was a child. It needed to stop.

The cab pulled up to the curb. I paid my former classmate, snatched up my bag, and went up to the door. The Ford's tires chirped pulling away. Shit, another enemy. How do I keep making enemies when all I want to do is fly below everyone's radar? People are mysterious to me.

I walked past a new Ford SUV in the driveway.

I knocked on the front door, and a few moments later, my grandfather answered it. "Yes?"

"It's me. Tris."

He blinked a few times. "You look like shit."

"Thanks."

"Why'd you knock?"

"Because I didn't want you to shoot me. You didn't even recognize me just now."

"It was the sun."

"We're under an overhang."

"It was the shade."

"May I come in?"

"Of course. That's what you're here for."

He opened the door wide for me and stepped aside. I walked into my old house. There was a scent to it, like someone had been doing serious pickling in there. I went back to my bedroom and dumped my bag on the bed. Nothing had changed since the last time I was here. The sameness was comforting.

I emerged from the bedroom and nearly walked into a woman dressed like she was about to perform surgery. She was my height, with artificially blonde hair tied up in a bun at the back. A surgical mask hung round her neck. Her makeup was laid on with a spackling knife. Or a trowel. Underneath all that makeup, she was in her late thirties, by my guesstimate. I also guessed that the impressive pair of breasts under the surgical getup were placed there by an actual surgeon. "Holy shit, Tris. You scared the hell out of me. Your grandfather told me you were on your way down."

"Hello."

"You don't remember me, do you?"

"No."

"We were in band together in high school. You played the clarinet."

"Of course I did."

"Kourtnee Lyons."

"Yes. Courteney."

"With a 'K' and ending with an 'e, e.'"

"It's the hair, maybe."

"Or maybe it's my boobs."

"They're hard to ignore."

"One of my clients had them installed when I was in a different profession."

"I won't ask."

"I was a sex worker."

I didn't know how to react. What are you supposed to say in that moment? I smiled politely. We were standing in a hallway outside my old bedroom, now my new bedroom, chatting for some damn reason. "You're taking care of my grandmother now."

"Yes, I'm her CNA. I work for hospice. It's tremendously challenging work."

"I bet it is."

"What are you doing these days?"

"I'm unemployed at the moment. It's unchallenging. May I go see her?"

"You're funny. You were always funny though. Remember that band trip, when we went up to New York City? How you chased down a cab? You got up on a stage at that one club and did a little routine."

"How could I forget?" I was never in band, I have never been to New York City, I did nothing in high school, joined no clubs, made no friends, yet every former classmate I ran into had vivid memories of me.

"Go on back. She's awake." Kourtnee patted me on the shoulder solicitously and walked away.

I crept back to the bedroom. I pushed open the door and it sang out a bit on creaky hinges. "Matka?" I half-whispered, peering in.

She was in bed, the sheets up to her chin, her mouth formed into a little oh. She opened her eyes and smacked her mouth. "Come here, come here," she implored.

I tiptoed over and sat on the straight-backed chair beside her bed.

"Come closer."

I moved the chair closer to the head of the bed. "Matka."

"Where have you been?"

"Away. I'm back now."

"Good, good. What about that woman? Is she with you?"

"Which one?"

"The homely one. The one you married."

"We divorced."

"Good, good." She smacked her lips. I reached over to a TV tray and picked up a water glass with a straw. I held it to her mouth and she sucked on the straw for a moment. "That's enough. Thank you." I put the glass back. She whispered, "Is that whore around?"

"The CNA? She's taking her break, I think."

"She's trying to steal your grandfather from me."

"I doubt that."

"The women. They love members of the party, no matter how old they are. Party members are strong. I was always a sucker for strong men."

"Pop is pretty old."

"He wants to fool around."

"I doubt that." I rummaged through my memories of Pop. I couldn't remember an instance when he seemed like he wanted to fool around. There was nothing fooling-around about him, save his adherence to doctrinaire communism.

"Ah, you don't know him."

"Epistemologically speaking, how can we know anyone, or anything? People and things outside of ourselves exist, but they make themselves manifest only in appearance, not as they are in and of themselves."

"You and your philosophy classes. Your books. Philosophy is a bunch of hooey. Come closer."

I leaned in. Her hand emerged from beneath the sheet and I took it in both of mine. Hard bones under soft skin. "Promise me that when the time comes, you'll pour that entire bottle of liquid morphine down my throat." Next to the water pitcher on the TV tray was a brown quart bottle of morphine.

"I don't know."

"Promise." She fixed me with a firm stare out of rheumy eyes.

"I promise."

"Good boy. You should eat something." She slipped her hand out of mine and closed her eyes.

I left the room and closed the door behind me. I stood frozen in the hallway outside her door. "This isn't real. None of this is real." I wept, standing there. I realized that Matka was the only person I ever truly loved, and it was because she had loved me unconditionally. I'd spent too much time away, and now there was no time left. I was expected to kill her with morphine when she gave the signal.

I went into the hallway bathroom, closed the door and washed my face. I looked around and no towel was in evidence. I looked under the sink and found, all the way in the back, a full, plastic bottle of cheap gin. I remembered putting it there years before. Something to nip on when the going wasn't going my way. I took a quick pull and put it back. I went out into the hall and found a towel in the hallway closet. I looked at the way it was folded and realized that LeeAnn must have folded it, that she must have washed all the towels and put them away when we were here that one time, when Matka had insulted her. I took out a hand towel and a bath towel and brought them into the bathroom. I held the bath towel up to my face, closed my eyes and sniffed deeply. There was no trace of LeeAnn on the towel. I told myself that I wasn't disappointed.

That reminds me. I need to swap out the hand towel and bath towel. And maybe wash my sheets. I haven't done that yet since I've been home.

I sat on the couch next to Kourtnee. My grandfather sat in his chair, reading *The Daily Worker*. The TV was silent.

"What should I be doing?" I asked aloud.

Pop ruffled the paper. "What?"

"What should I be doing? What do you need me to do?"

"Kourtnee's got it handled," he said.

"I've got it handled. It's comfort stuff now. We're keeping her comfortable."

"We're keeping her comfortable," Pop said.

"Comfortable."

"I just said that," Pop said.

"Your grandfather and I—"

"Later!"

"No, he needs to hear it now, Joe."

"Joe," I went. "She calls you 'Joe.'"

"He needs to hear it from you. *I* need to hear it from you. Say it, Joe."

"Yes, 'Joe.' Say it," I said.

He lowered the paper. "We mean to get married."

"Married," I went.

"Do you need to get your ears cleaned out? Yes, married. Kourtnee and I."

"But—"

"He's about to say something ageist, Joe."

"Don't be ageist, boy."

"Can't you support our love?" Kourtnee reached over and touched my hand.

"Oh for God's sake." I pulled my hand away.

"Typical of a capitalist to bring his imaginary friend into it."

"He means 'God.' Your grandfather and I expect you to get a job. Pull your weight."

"My grandfather made me quit my job and move down here because he said he was lonely. That was clearly a lie."

"*Made* you? Pfft! Look, we need a little time off. For ourselves," Pop said. "I figured we could take a trip. See the sights. Your grandmother will be fine right here while you look after her."

"So Kourtnee doesn't have it handled? And fine? She has terminal cancer. She's never going to be fine." The discordant noise emanating from the center of my brain raised to a crescendo. I felt a slight pop in the middle of my chest, and deflated, and the noise tapered off a bit. "And suddenly, it all becomes clear." I leaned back on the couch. I was done being angry. Some vital circuitry deep in my brain burned out.

"You don't seem angry," Kourtnee said irritably. "Or surprised." She seemed slightly angry and slightly surprised that I wasn't angry or surprised.

"I'm neither. You two go have a good time elsewhere. I'll hold down the fort. I'll take care of Matka. I have it handled as of right now. She took care of me."

They looked at each other, and then back at me, then at each other again.

Both Kourtnee's anger and surprise at my lack of anger or surprise soon passed, replaced by relief. She said, "Okay then."

Pop said, "Okay then." He went back to reading *The Daily Worker*.

She clicked on the tube.

"What's the most dangerous vegetable? Stay tuned to *The Guy Morton Show* to find out from our medical expert, Doctor Boaz!"

I went back to the master bedroom to be with my grandmother, sat in the straight-backed chair again. I felt myself nodding off. I got up, walked to a corner of the room and fell asleep sitting with my back against the wall.

The night nurse shook me awake and I went back out into the living room. My grandfather was asleep in his chair. Kourtnee was watching a prime-time talk show hosted by a former English soccer player turned verbally abusive restaurant chef. A soothsayer named the Blind Dutchman was led onto the set by a pair of women dressed up like Las Vegas showgirls. The Blind Dutchman was bald with a goatee, wearing a turtleneck sweater. His eyes consisted only of whites. Once the Blind Dutchman was seated, he informed the audience in a tremulous, deep voice, "I will now go into a trance. I must not be disturbed during my trance, otherwise I will disappear into the netherworld, never to return. I require complete silence." The studio lights dimmed, save for a lone blue spotlight trained down on the Blind Dutchman from above. The camera zoomed in until his blue face filled the screen. An audience member coughed. The Blind Dutchman slipped into an apparent trance, his fluttering hands raised shoulder high, and warbled importantly: "A post-apocalyptic event will take place at a romantic parking lot. Images, GIFs and videos will be featured seven times a day. Travel advice. Travel tips. All within your grasp. Simple eats and mezcal. It's time for unwilted thinking. It's time to experience comfort and satisfaction. The year is 1971. The place? A truly unusual indoor seafood restaurant, located in the convenience of your favorite mall near the food court, operated by a hospitality collective. Savory bite-size smelts for the eyes, nose and soul, plus an addictive chemical, a meta-mix of voice memos, taped conversations and come-to-Jesus moments—a mixture of character, quality and consistency. Level One. Free-skiing. Five percent pleasure. One hundred twenty percent effort. Interweave, braid, plait, entwine, intertwine, interlace, knit, mesh... marry. You got it, bro. You got this. You're feeling sleepy. Sleepy." His hands lowered, his head tilted down, and he seemed to fall asleep in his chair. The house lights turned back up. He blinked awake. Applause thundered out to the sniffing disapproval of the soccer player turned malevolent chef, who glared into the camera and snapped out, "We'll be right back!" The show cut to a commercial for a chain seafood restaurant at Sarasota Square Mall.

"We should go to dinner," Kourtnee said.

"Okay."

"A late dinner. Wouldn't that be nice? The three of us? We could all get reacquainted."

"Yes."

"I'll wake up Joe."

"Sure."

We stood at the sign that said, PLEASE WAIT TO BE SEATED, waiting to be seated. Pop glared around at the room, filled with contempt. The mall itself filled him with rage, even though the mall was dying. Two of the three anchor department stores were empty, their signs pried off, leaving what appeared to be a shadow of their names behind. A yellow banner with black lettering on each store announced, SPACE AVAILABLE FOR RENT. The third anchor store had a banner on the outside that read, EVERYTHING IN STORE 70 PERCENT OFF. GOING OUT OF BUSINESS SALE. Inside the mall, most of the stores were shuttered, with optimistic messages on their exteriors about how a new business would be coming soon. The most common sign was FIND YOUR PAR-ADISE, which featured a beach scene. The few people inside the mall wandered around with their phones out, documenting the end of the mall, or checking for mes-sages while getting their walking done in an air-condi-tioned environment.

Finally, an employee dressed in all black, like some sort of service industry Johnny Cash, asked us if we had reservations. I peered around at the empty restaurant for a moment before saying, "No."

"That's okay," he said, checking a list on the podium. "I think I can find you a table. Three?"

"Yes," I said. "Three."

"Follow me."

We followed him through the restaurant, which was far more vast than it looked from the food court entrance, to a back section filled with elderly people. They sat poking at the gelid remains of fish on their plates, conversing in tired voices with an occasional high-pitched cackle, sucking in oxygen from Jacques Cousteau contraptions on wheels next to them, their three-wheeled scooters parked next to the tables.

"Look at all these parasites," Pop said to no one in particular.

"They're retirees," I said.

"They retired the day they were born," he replied. "Leeches sucking the lifeblood of the workingman."

"And here we are!" Johnny Cash pulled out a seat for Kourtnee, and Pop sat down in it. So Johnny Cash pulled out a second seat and Kourtnee sat down. "It's so nice to see three generations of a family together."

Kourtnee started to correct him. "We're not—"

"Thank you. My daughter takes such good care of me and my father," I said.

"Have a great meal," Johnny Cash said, handing us menus.

"Why did you do that?" Kourtnee asked me after the man in black departed our company.

"We'll get better service if we have a heartwarming backstory."

"Lies! The entire system they set up is filled with lies." Pop flipped through the menu furiously. "This isn't even food. Boiled potatoes and carrots with meat beside it. That's food. What the hell is a 'flying fish roe cream cheese salmon tart'? Or 'dried pork and seaweed crusted lime grouper'? It's exploitation, that's what it is! We're throwing away the sweat of our labor."

Kourtnee and I looked at each other for a moment. "You're such a good daughter for putting up with your granddad and me in a public setting." I patted her hand, which she pulled away.

"We discussed it while you were in with your grandmother. We're leaving tomorrow."

"Good. Don't let the door hit you on your considerable backside on your way out."

"You can be angry if you want. It's okay." Kourtnee reached over and patted my hand.

"I choose to be happy for my cheating grandfather who couldn't wait for my dying grandmother to be put in the ground so he could run off with a former stripper."

"Sex worker," Pop said. "That's the preferred nomenclature for those who are systematically exploited by ruling class males in the sex trades." He set the menu aside.

"Know what you want?" Kourtnee asked him.

"Meat and potatoes," Pop said. "Or an apple with cheese."

"How about you?" she asked me.

"A quart of vodka, in honor of your forthcoming nuptials." I sat back in my chair. "It's all so cheery. My very own daughter, finally getting married to my very own father. I could weep with joy."

Kourtnee gave me a stern look. "That stopped being funny five minutes ago."

"I'll let you know when it stops being funny." I peered around. "Where's the waiter? Let's light this candle."

It was a good thing that Kourtnee drove. By the time we were ready to leave, the waiter had cut me off from a succession of vodka gimlets and whiskey sours. I was stumbling drunk. I almost walked directly into an elderly man on my way out of the restaurant. He was being led by Johnny Cash back to the section where we'd been seated. The elderly man was dressed in mismatched clothes from 20 years ago. He was using an aluminum walker with beige grips that had a basket from child's bicycle attached to the front. The basket was filled with artificial flowers. He stared ahead solemnly, past me, past everything, perhaps into that blue tunnel that dying people see. He was going forward and nothing would get in his way. Certainly not a balding drunk in khakis and a black pocket t-shirt.

We backtracked through the mall on our way to wherever the hell Kourtnee had parked. The thing that is striking when I'm away from Florida for an extended period of time is how many old people populate the Sunshine State. I felt young. Or youngish. So many aluminum walkers. So many motorized conveyances. So many oxygen cans on wheels. So much white hair and angry sullen stares. It was a refreshing change of pace from Chicago, where it seemed like I was always the oldest person in the room. Or at least the oldest *looking* person.

I walked up to an elderly couple. "Hello. I'm running for mayor. Vote for me." I shook their hands.

"You're drunk!" the blue hair informed me.

"We all should be drunk. Every one of us."

"I'm sorry," Kourtnee said, pulling me away. "His grandmother is dying."

"They don't need to know that," I snapped. "They don't need to know anything."

The old couple scooted away.

"You should be kind. Treat people the way you want to be treated," Kourtnee said.

"Oh, is that what you learned down at the old strip club?"

"Don't be mean," she said.

"I don't believe in the categorical imperative. Obviously. I skimmed *Groundwork of the Metaphysics of Morals* for just that reason. So I could disagree with it."

"You're a coward. You're hiding behind your intellectualism."

"Pfft!" I went. "Clearly."

She grabbed my upper arm with her left hand. She was stunningly strong. She dragged me along in the mall while Pop toddled along beside her.

I threw up in the parking lot under a mercury vapor lamp. Dead bugs littered the cracked and pot-holed blacktop. The nighttime hum of insects and birds filled the air. I could hear an alligator croaking somewhere. The wet air smelled like death.

I fell asleep in the car going home and awoke in my bed the next morning, my body and mouth sour and reeking. I took a shower and put on a fresh t-shirt and underwear. My khakis were dirty, so I tossed them in the corner of my room. I found another pair of khakis in my closet and put those on. I velcroed my shoes onto my feet and wandered out into the living room. I found a tented note in the kitchen. TRIS. I picked it up and read on the inside.

"After your atrocious behavior last night, we decided to leave early this morning. Will see you when we get back. Kourtnee. P.S. Please try to take better care of yourself."

"You don't rule me," I said, crumpling up the note. I tossed it in the kitchen garbage can, which was full of the burnt remains of potato wedges, like someone had kept making them and burning them, going through the process over and over and still not getting it right. There had to be the remains of at least ten pounds of potatoes in there. I hefted the full bag outside and tossed it in the waste disposal company-issued plastic garbage can on wheels on the concrete pad next to the central air conditioner.

I went back inside and checked the beer situation out in the fridge. Pop had laid in a full supply of Natty Light, so I was good to go.

The doorbell rang, so I answered it. A woman in pink scrubs stood there. "I'm the new CNA from hospice," she said.

I stepped out of her way, and back she went. I followed her.

She took my grandmother's pulse. She shook the brown bottle. "Was this full or empty yesterday?"

"Full, I think."

"It's empty now. Did you give her all this?"

"No."

"She must have taken it herself."

"What are you saying?"

"I'm saying she has no pulse. She may have passed on."

"May have?"

"You can say goodbye. I'm calling our doctor. He'll be here in a half hour. You can sit with her."

"Okay."

"Where's the husband?"

"He left."

"When will he be back?"

"I don't know."

"You should call him. You should let him know."

"Give me a minute."

"Take all the time you need." She left the room. I heard her talking in the other room a moment later.

I sat down in the straight-backed chair. I took Matka's unresisting hand into mine. She was cold. "I'm sorry." It was too late for that. I should have apologized the day before. "I'm sorry. I love you."

The next two hours were a blur. Matka had made arrangements to be cremated and for the ashes to be dumped at sea. There was no funeral. A doctor arrived and declared her dead. An ambulance arrived and I watched the two attendants zip her into a black bag, place the bag on a gurney, and take her body away. I signed things that were handed to me on clipboards. More people came and took away all the things that hospice had brought. Soon, it was like Matka hadn't been there at all.

I wandered around the house. I took down all of my grade school portraits and placed them in a box. I put the box in the garage. I drank. I went back to bed.

My phone rang, waking me up. The caller ID said, US GOVERNMENT. I answered it.

"This is Hank," a familiar voice said. "I thought you should hear this from me."

"Hank," I said. "My... my grandmother is dead." The moment I said it, it became real. I broke down crying.

"Jesus." Hank waited for me to calm down. When I stopped sobbing, Hank asked, "Are you still there?"

"Yes," I said, my voice cracking.

"Your grandfather is dead, too."

"What?" I went. "What?"

"He and his girlfriend were hit head-on by a cross-country bus. The driver fell asleep at the wheel, crossed a median and four lanes of traffic."

"What?"

"I claimed the body. I've known your grandfather for most of three decades without formally meeting him. It was the least I could do."

"Did you—?"

"I saw the whole thing. I was fifteen car-lengths behind him. I was being discreet in accordance with bureau guidelines." He stopped speaking.

I had nothing to say.

"Tris, I'm going to need you to be strong. I'll be there with the remains tomorrow."

"Remains."

"Your grandfather wished to be cremated. So I'm having him cremated here tonight. Then I'll drive back down. Should be there by late afternoon."

"Where are you?"

"Valdosta, Georgia."

"Georgia. They made good time."

"That nurse's assistant liked speeding. I'll see you tomorrow." The phone clicked dead.

I drank up most of the Natty Light and went back to bed.

I awoke, blinking my eyes. Hank was standing at the foot of my bed. He was holding a jumbo can of Folger's. "You brought me coffee?"

"It's your grandfather."

I sat up and rubbed my eyes. "In a coffee can?"

"I felt obligated to have him cremated. Not so much on buying a fancy urn. Figured he wouldn't appreciate the urn either. Remember that movie with the bowlers in it?"

"Um."

He set the urn down on my bureau. "Got sloshed, did you?"

"Yes."

"Get up and I'll make you some breakfast."

"That's okay."

"I'll make some coffee. I have a big plastic bag full of it out in the car."

"Folger's?"

"Uh, huh." He left. I got up and put on my clothes. I scooped up Pop's cremains and took it with me out into the living room. I sat for a moment on my spot on the couch, staring off into space.

Hank came back in with a sack of groceries. He took off his suit-coat and tossed it on Pop's chair. He rolled up his sleeves and started to make breakfast.

"He wouldn't want to be in a can with a corporate logo," I said.

"No, I suppose not," Hank said, pulling out an iron skillet.

"I'll be right back." I went out into the garage and found a can of spray paint. I spritzed the Folger's can until it was primer gray. I watched the can dry. The scent of breakfast wafted out into the garage. I wondered what had happened to Matka's Ford Ranchero. Pop probably sold it when it became clear that she'd never drive again. I left Pop's cremains on the garage floor and went inside.

Hank and I sat in the dining room. I watched him eat a full breakfast. "Sure you don't want any of this?"

I drank the coffee he'd poured for me. "Positive. Thanks for bringing him back."

"I didn't think you'd be able to."

"Yeah. You're right about that."

The doorbell rang, so I got up to answer it. A group of dour white men stood outside. There were maybe 20 of them. The street was full of parallel-parked cars, all of them old and pockmarked with rust. The young ones wore t-shirts with Che Guevara. The old ones wore drab suits and gray ties, the only color on them being a red star on the lapel.

"We've come to pay our respects," the man closest to the door said.

"Come in." I led them into the living room and they sat on the couch, on his chair, in Matka's chair, and stood around in the kitchen. They'd brought nothing with them for the wake but their grief. I went out into the garage and picked up the coffee can, which had completely dried. On a hunch, I opened the garage door and saw Hank walking from car to car, taking pictures of license plates. He raised a shushing finger to his mouth. I closed the garage door and went back inside. I set the can down on the kitchen counter. They each filed past the can, solemnly touching it and moving on. As they walked out the front door, Hank took photos of them from his government sedan across the street. After the last man departed, I stood on the front porch and looked into Hank's camera as he snapped a final shot of me. I waved goodbye to him. He put away his camera and drove up to the curb. He summoned me over.

"It's the end of an era," he said.

"Thank you for bringing him back."

"What will you do now?"

"He always wanted to go to Cuba. So I figured I'd mail him to the Cuban embassy."

"I mean *you*. What will *you* do now?"

"I don't know. But that's not new. I never know."

"Please try to take care of yourself."

"You know I won't."

"Yeah. I know you won't." He drove away.

I'm almost finished with my story, so stop looking at me like that. Eat a donut. They're full of sugar, and possibly vitamins. Have some coffee. Me, I'll finish off what I have in my flask and then mosey along.

Now where was I? Right.

Bubby woke me up. What he did was stand on my chest and make a sound like a pissed off duck, which is frightening when you're coming out of a bender-based sleep. "Qweee!" he went, flailing his furry little arms.

"Aaah!" I went, flailing my much larger arms. I'd passed out on the sofa. The doorbell was ringing. Someone was really standing on the thing. Then there was some pounding with a flattened hand on the door, like a deputy sheriff was on the other side of the door ready to evict me. Bubby hopped off my chest and lumped over to his spot on the counter. "Let's see who that is, shall we?"

I staggered over to the door and flung it open. LaShonda was standing there in huff. "We're in trouble," she said, pushing past me to come inside.

"Oh?" I went innocently.

"That raccoon is government property. We got a cease and desist letter by courier this morning. Some Navy JAG on Navy letterhead, and all signed off by a Navy captain."

"Now look who's calling him, 'that raccoon.' Your lack of sensitivity is disturbing."

"Don't be cute this morning, Tris." She turned and sniffed at my face. "You smell like a brewery."

"I *am* a brewery. I'm temporarily not filled with beer. I intend to rectify that situation as soon as humanly possible."

"Where is he?"

"Are you referring to 'that raccoon'? If so, he's in the kitchen." We walked into the kitchen to find that "that raccoon" had made me into a liar. "Quite possibly, he's made his escape."

"That wouldn't be the most tragic thing he could do." LaShonda bit her lip contemplatively. "Maybe it's for the best."

I heard the toilet flushing. "Or maybe he just took an enormous shit. He ate a lot at that football game the other day. Shoveled it in with both of his furry little hands. When was that? Was it yesterday? Or the day before yesterday? I'm losing track. It's been such a whirlwind."

"Shut up. Give me a second to think."

"Thinking has never done me one bit of good in this life." I thought for a moment. "And not thinking hasn't done me much good either." I checked out the beer situation in the fridge. It was not promising. I picked up my phone intending to order a case of beer and a crunchwrap supreme. I was out of minutes and I had no WiFi. I tried signing in again to the neighbor's, but he'd changed his password. Foiled! "You got any cash on you? I have to make a beer run."

"That ship has sailed," LaShonda said. "So you can stop showing me your empty palm."

I lowered my hand.

Bubby came staggering out and was immediately cheered by the sight of his lawyer. He galloped over and attached himself to her leg. She gave him a kick across the room. He tumbled near my grandfather's chair and climbed up into it, unfazed by her rough treatment. "Oochy, oochy," he went.

"Now I've got a run in my stocking." She was wearing a skirt-type suit, all black with coffee-colored pantyhose. She was quite fetching, not that I was attempting to notice. "Great, now the drunk is checking out my legs. This is a fantastic day."

The doorbell rang again.

"Well, shit. I shouldn't have worried that I was becoming unpopular. All sorts of people are beating down my door."

"I'm not here." LaShonda scurried off into the hallway. I heard the master bedroom door close. If she put a water glass up to the wall in the master bath, she'd be able to listen in. Heck, she wouldn't even need the water glass. The walls were paper-thin.

I opened the front door and found a pair of Navy officers dressed head to toe in khaki standing there. One was the pinch-faced captain who I'd spoken to the day before. She couldn't have been much over five-feet tall. The other one was a smirking homecoming king who was at least a foot taller than his companion. He took off his mirrored aviator glasses. "How do?"

"Fair to middling. I take it you're here for my furry friend."

"You haven't made friends with him, have you?" Captain Novak asked, a bit worried.

"There's nothing wrong with that raccoon. I find him charming, dear," Commander McCrae said. "Mind if we come in?"

I stepped out of their way. "Be my guest."

"Of course you'd find a genetically enhanced raccoon charming," Captain Novak said, stepping past me into my home. "After the lab accident, it has to be like looking into a mirror."

"I don't look like a raccoon," Commander McCrae said, following his wife. "You're being hurtful, darling."

"That's one opinion," Captain Novak said. "There are other opinions, most of them mine, which have more validity." She turned and stopped him with a held-up hand. "You stay here. Remember what happened last time you confronted him."

Commander McCrae looked mournfully at me. "He freaked out a bit. Kept shouting out, 'No! No!'" He did a passable Bubby impression. "Watched the videos yesterday before we had them all deleted. I'm a fan. He's a much better dancer than the old ball-and-chain."

"I'm an excellent dancer! Ask anyone!" Captain Novak barked at him.

"Last time we went dancing, someone tried to stick a wallet in her mouth."

"That is clearly a fabrication." She turned her attention to me. "Well?"

"He's in the living room. I'll take you to him." I walked ahead of her to where Bubby was seated on the couch, and then stepped out of her way.

She sat down next to him and patted him on the head. Bubby went, "Au-dee."

"I'm going to take you home, okay? We'll make this right."

"Au-dee."

"I know this is hard for you to understand, but you're not Bobby McCrae. You're a genetically enhanced raccoon that I was trying to teach sign language."

"Bubby Muck."

"It was a lab accident. We were trying to project Bobby's memories from himself in the present to himself in the past. Just a few memories transmitted on a wave of antimatter. But it kind of went awry and you got all of his memories. I know you don't understand, but that's the truth."

"Bubby. Bubby Muck."

"Do you trust me?"

"Noooo."

"Attaboy. Anyway, it's time to go." Like a magic trick, she suddenly had a small, metallic pistol in her right hand. She placed it at the base of his skull and I heard a pneumatic pop.

Bubby eyes rolled and he slumped, asleep.

"That's it then," I said.

"That's it." Captain Novak stood up. "You understand you shouldn't talk about this, right?"

"Who'd believe me?"

"No one. That's why you shouldn't talk about it. If you'd read the comments on your YouTube page, you'd have noticed one thing... no one believes the evidence of their own eyes when it comes to the fantastic. They'd rather believe in a cynical untruth." She clucked her tongue. "Did we mention that we had you banned from YouTube and your page deleted? Well, anyway, that happened. No offense intended."

I shrugged. "None taken. Are you going to vivisect him?"

"I could lie to you and say no."

"I'd rather you lie to me."

"Your raccoon friend is going to live a long and productive life."

"Thank you."

"You're welcome." She attempted to smile and failed. She reached out and we shook hands. "I'm sorry about all this."

"I wasn't doing much with my life anyway. Drinking, mostly."

"Yes, I read up on you. My father was an alcoholic, I'm told. He killed himself a long time ago, when I was a little girl. His death has colored my life all this time." She grimaced at the memory of her lost father. "There's no one you care for? No one who cares for you?"

"They're all gone. It's just me and the bottle."

"I'm sorry to hear that. Don't drink and drive."

"I've done enough vehicular homicide in my life. Enough damage. I don't even own a car. Haven't in a long time."

"If you'd like to check into a clinic—"

"I'm good."

"I don't think you are."

"Please take your raccoon and go."

Captain Novak turned her head. "Bobby!"

"Coming, dear." The much taller man appeared in the living room. He peered over at the sleeping raccoon. "I'll carry him out to the gov-vee. Stick him in the cage we brought."

"That sounds like a marvelous plan, Bobby. Did you bring the check?"

"Yes." He reached into a pocket and retrieved a folded-in-half check and handed it to me. "Here you go, ace."

I unfolded it. It was made out to me from the United States Government for $11,145 and no cents. "Thank you."

"That's for retrieving government property," Captain Novak said. "Don't spend it all in one place."

"I'll try not to."

Commander McCrae scooped up the sleeping creature and held him like a baby in his arms. "It's a shame that we'll have to—"

"Shhh!" She thumbed over at me. "He's attached."

"Take him to that wonderful farm. Such a beautiful farm."

"Yes. Beautiful farm." Captain Novak arched her eyebrows at me. "Goodbye, Mister Edgar. We'll see ourselves out."

LaShonda appeared at my side. She snatched the check out of my hand. "This should be enough."

"Enough?"

"I'm going to take you to a clinic. You're going to sober up."

I started to say something, but felt a familiar rumbling coming from my guts. Before I could rush to the sink, or anywhere, a torrent of blood came gushing from my mouth and landed on LaShonda's skirt.

She shrieked and jumped back. "My God!" Her face was contorted with disgust. And then came the concern. The pity. "I'm calling an ambulance."

"I'm fine." I wiped my mouth with the back of my hand.

"You're not fine."

I wanted to argue with her. But I felt lightheaded. The last thing I remember before waking up here at the get-sober hospital was the floor coming up to meet with my face in a not-so-gentle manner.

I'm willing to take questions.

Anyone? Hello?

Yes, you in the back.

The question was, "Are you completely crazy?" What kind of question is that, I ask you? If I was completely crazy, would I be able to stand up here and hold your attention for all this time? Of course not. So let's just say that I'm incompletely crazy and leave it at that.

Yes, the lady with the pink "I Heart My Dachshund" t-shirt on.

The question was, "Is this some sort of a test?" Ma'am, life is some sort of a test. I would hazard a guess that we've all failed that test and that's why we're here.

Yes, the man who ate most of the donuts.

The question was, "Where the hell was the raccoon while Carwyn was visiting?"

First, thank you for paying attention. Second, it's funny you should ask that, because in preparation for coming out here, I went through various and sundry social media feeds, including that of Sharma-LeenXXX, the sleepy-eyed star of Instagram, and other solipsistic folks. Here's the story I was able to piece together from those various feeds.

Just hear me out, one last time. I swear that I'm not making this up, that I'm not just a well-lubricated gasbag.

After napping off his titanic meal from the game, a miffed Bubby made his way out to the site of the plane crash.

He rode a garbage truck out there. Have you seen that YouTube video shot from the window of someone's car? You should look it up.

After Bubby arrived at the crash site, he capered in front of every camera he could find, but the cameras turned off. His story had ended. His second act would never arrive.

Sharm-LeenXXX herself told him that, in a rare speaking appearance in front of a camera. She told him that her days were numbered as well.

"Suh-sad," Bubby said.

"It's not so sad," Sharma-LeenXXX said. "I've saved a lot of money. I've put it into a mix of municipal bonds and treasury bonds. I was accepted into USC. You know, the one out in California? I'm going to major in finance. Maybe I'll get a job as an agent and help other people like me manage their money. I could help you, if you were human."

"No muh-money," Bubby said. "Duh-dumb hyoo-human has money."

"He's an alcoholic. I could smell it on him, like an overripe nectarine, you know? He won't last long." She looked into the camera, addressing me. "Sorry, dude. But we both know it's the truth."

She put Bubby into a gypsy cab, with a shabby driver wearing an FSU hoodie.

He shot the cab ride with a phone aimed over his shoulder. "What's up, critter? Where we going, amigo?" But he already knew where he was going. Everyone knew.

Bubby sulked in the back seat, sliding back and forth at every turn and every tap of the brakes.

He let Bubby off at the end of the street. Bubby hopped out of the cab, where three miscreant children awaited him with rocks. They pelted him and shot it with their phones at the same time.

Bubby picked up a knife that had been tossed at him, waved it at the children, who backed off, and made his escape into the retention pond.

The next bit of film I saw was from a neighbor's early morning walk. It was shot from far off. Bubby stood over the corpse of the alligator that had made the retention pond his home. Bubby's paws were covered in blood. He gasped for breath. The knife was plunged into the head of the alligator, between the eyes.

Another resident of our neighborhood shot more phone video of Bubby swimming in her pool.

Did that answer your question?

Ah, the attendants have arrived. And, hey, does everyone remember LaShonda? From my story? There she is right there. Hello, LaShonda! Wave to everyone. She's not waving.

I'm hoping she's here to tell me that Doug Liberty has bought the rights to my life and that my new name is "Doug Liberty Presents Tris Edgar the Shitty Ex-Husband and Drunk." She's shaking her head no. Ain't that a kick in the pants?

I would like to mention that I wasn't brought up in any faith group, in case you're wondering about my stance on the almighty and the hereafter. I hope there isn't a hereafter. I hope that life is finite. I believe that it is.

I like to think of myself as being like a saint however. My favorite was Saint Simeon Stylites. He tied a belt around his midsection so tightly that it caused his flesh to decompose. He became infested with worms. When the worms would fall off him, he would put them back on his decaying flesh and tell them, "Eat up! Eat what God's given you!" That's my kind of faith.

Do we have souls? Of course not. That would mean that once I'm done with this greasy, ill-made wreck of a body, I'll still be stuck existing. I can't accept that. I won't.

I think people are merely complex machines made of meat. We're programmed via beatings, feedings, TV and hugs in our early years by other meat machines, usually the meat machines that created us and bestowed upon us their genetics and thus the wiring for our sad brains.

Once we leave home, we bounce around life like a pinball, from one hazard to the next, pretending that we have choices as we're pushed and paddled this way and that.

What I'm describing here is called "physical determinism," which can trace its origins all the way back to the Epicureans. Feel free to discuss this concept after I've quit the podium. If any of you decide to argue for compatibilism, I'm afraid I'll have to clock you with this mostly empty flask.

A common fantasy for most human beings is thinking about what they should have done differently years before and how wonderful their lives would be if only they hadn't made that one horrible choice. Here's the thing I don't think they understand: They didn't have a choice when they made the choice. The programming inside their heads determined the choice. We're all nothing but hormones, genetics and remembered childhood beatings. There isn't a soul, untouched by meat, that is guiding us around with an invisible joystick. There is no Cartesian mind-body problem. Descartes was full of shit.

If I see myself as a meat machine, then why can't I forgive myself for killing my family as a child? After all, that was the kind of machine I was at the time. A killing machine. The answer is, of course, that I am not a self-forgiving machine. You're welcome.

We've done amazing things as a species despite our programming—like going to the moon, for instance. We're also doomed to pollute and bomb our planet to death, because that's also the type of meat machines that we are. We can't help ourselves.

No one is coming to save us from ourselves either. I'm sorry to report that Santa, ancient aliens and Jesus are not on their way. That's another common human fantasy.

In closing—and I'm really finished at this point because, as you can clearly see, the attendants are making their way to the podium—I'd like to quote an OG philosopher, Aristotle, who said, "I count him braver who overcomes his desires than him who conquers his enemies, for the hardest victory is over self."

There is no victory over self. I've proven that, I think, gleefully. Goodbye!

About the author

Born in Cleveland, Ohio in 1963 under a cloud of industrial pollution, John L. Sheppard grew up in Florida and attended the University of Florida, where he received an MFA in 1994. He lives in Illinois. If you've heard of him, it's probably because he wrote the novel *Small Town Punk*.